PECKED TO DE

D1633935

. . . OR

MURDER UNDER THE PRARIE CHICKEN

Pecked to Death

...Or...

Murder Under the Prarie Chicken

Gerald Anderson

North Star Press of St. Cloud, Inc.
St. Cloud, Minnesota

"To the people, past and present, of Highland Grove. Highland Grove is in eastern Clay County, Minnesota, and is very probably the site of the original Garden of Eden."

Published by
North Star Press of St. Cloud, Inc.
P.O. Box 451
St. Cloud, Minnesota 56302

northstarpress.com

PROLOGUE

THE KILLER WAS INEXPERIENCED.

"So this is what it feels like to kill somebody. Huh! I don't feel any different than I did five minutes ago. In fact, I don't feel anything at all. How can I be so calm? I'm completely sane. Still, I suppose if I were completely sane, I wouldn't be talking to myself. Who else am I going to talk to? I suppose I could talk to the stiff, but I have a feeling he wouldn't be amusing company. That's kind of funny, he-he-he-he. Wait a minute. I'm giggling. I never giggle. Get a grip. Now, what would that expired lump of protoplasm say to me? 'Why did you kill me? That was totally unnecessary.' And I would patiently explain, 'Well, that's the way it is,' using that ultimate bit of wisdom passed on every night by Walter Kronkite. 'Do you remember Walter Kronkite, Mr. Corpse?' Walter Kronkite could now report a murder. '. . . And in Fergus Falls, Minnesota, a body was found with his head bashed in with a crowbar. The perpetrator of this monstrosity is still at large.' Ah, I can hear him now.

"But you know, I can't let anybody find you here. No, I must take you away before they come to take me away, he-he-he-he. Now, what shall you wear. We don't want you leaving DNA samples all over the trunk of my car, now, do we? A blanket? No, they're always tracing fibers on those television shows. I suppose I could take off all of your clothes, but I presume your nude little body would leave traces and, besides, that would be so impolite. I've already been far too rude by hitting you over the head with my crow bar. Do you know why they call it a crow bar? Well, I don't either. If you get hit with one, you certainly aren't going to 'crow' about it, are you?

"I suppose I could wrap you up in newspapers like a neat mummy. I'd use lots of tape and save the funny papers until the very end—they'd make a nice scarf, don't you think? Oops, I forgot, you aren't talking, are you?

"Let's see, what would you like? Aha! Perfect. For death, you should dress in black, and what do we have here? A nice black plastic thirty-gallon garbage bag, perfect for dead leaves and dead persons. I will use two —one for your little feet and one for your little head.

You know, you really don't weigh all that much do you? Believe me, you'll weigh less in the coming years. In you go . . . And now for the lovely coat. There, don't you look all formal.

"Now, come on over and hop into my trunk. Oops, sorry, I didn't mean to tease. You can't hop, can you? You're so dead. Well, I'll give you a hand—in fact, I'll give you a whole round of applause. Yea, Corpsie, rah rah rah. O, my God, I'm cracking up."

He deposited his somewhat unwieldy bundle in the trunk and climbed behind the wheel. Without a clear plan of action, the car seemed to want to head over to the interstate. Within a mile he looked at the speedometer and noticed that he was going one hundred five miles per hour.

"Getting caught speeding with a body in the trunk would not be wise," the killer reasoned, as he slowed and rolled down the window to take in fresh clean April air.

"Ah! Invigorating! Just what I needed. Now what do I do? The first thing is to get rid of my friend in the back." At that moment, he saw a sign—"Exit 38, Rothsay, one mile." "Hey, back there, how does Rothsay sound to you?"

CHAPTER ONE

WORDSWORTH HAD IT ALL WRONG, for the Minnesota prairie, at least. April was not the cruelest month—that distinction belonged to March. Record cold temperatures for the month were more than thirty below zero, while the high temperatures could reach almost eighty. In the four-day blizzard of March 1966, winds reached almost one hundred miles an hour, and there were snow drifts thirty feet high. When the streets were plowed out, people put flags on the top of their radio antennas so that their cars could be seen at intersections.

And yet, there were years when the snow was gone by the middle of the month, and farmers were able to begin preparing their fields before April. Children, slaves to primers printed in less hostile climes, dutifully colored kites, and, if it were an early Easter, read about hunting for eggs in the grass. Hah! Hunting for Easter eggs would be easy in Minnesota. Colors have a way of standing out against white snow. And who would trust a delicate kite to the savage winds of a Minnesota March? Put one of those flimsy things into a Minnesota wind and it would immediately be reduced to splinters that would impale overly optimistic migratory birds, and it would probably serve them right! Even the most naive Pollyanna found March disgusting, depressing, vicious, contradictory, deceitful, nasty, brutish and long.

It didn't help to take a weekend in Minneapolis or Saint Paul, either. Go there in March and you find yourself in a hotel with hordes of adolescents, cheering, chanting, and—for all but a lucky few—crying. It is state tournament time, when thousands of busses are filled with teenagers released from their schools to scatter like stampeding bison through the downtowns or the Mall of America. There were tournaments in wrestling, girls and boys basketball, and girls and boys hockey. There seemed to be thousands of them—the Pied Piper of Hamelin manqué. More than likely, this event coincided with the last blizzard of the season, and raucous pre-adults shivered without the parkas their parents had implored them to take.

And yet, in the corner of the minds of many Minnesotans, something reminded them of how it felt to be fifteen and seeing for the first time the big city and William's Arena at the University of Minnesota. Perhaps going to some state tournament coincided with their first night spent in a hotel, but even then, sleeping was for the long bus ride home. And the Twin Cities in March? Well, if you lived two hundred miles away, coming south that far seemed close to going to Miami. Besides, it was only once a year.

All in all, March was a month to get through, something to be tolerated though intolerable. About the only thing to do was read seed catalogs and dream of the future. This was exactly what the members of the Otter Tail Bird Watching and Conservation Society were attempting to do.

Against all odds, the evening of March 16th was clear and calm, and although the temperature was only seven degrees, it was not impossible to dream of spring. The OTBWACS—the non-melodious acronym of the organization—had reserved a room at the Otter Tail County Historical Society for their monthly meeting. Supposedly, there were twenty-two members in the organization, but, no doubt because the Fergus Falls High School Otters were playing in the regional finals— just one step from the state tournament—only about half were present. Nevertheless, at precisely seven o'clock, they were called to order by their president, Carolyn Dahl.

Mrs. Dahl, widow of the late Dr. Donald Dahl, liked to keep active. Besides her interests in "Birding," she sang in the choir of Messiah Lutheran Church, arranged Meals on Wheels, served on the Otter Tail County Library Board, and organized the annual "10K Run for a Healthy Heart." Her late husband would foam at the mouth whenever the subject of socialized medicine came up and, seeing the surest preventative to be the Republican Party, had purchased influence with hefty donations. Carolyn, who had not had strong political convictions, became impatient with the incompetence of the local party organization, and was soon largely running it. On the death of "Doctor Dahlar," however, she began to become uneasy with the anti-feminist agenda of the party, and had simply stopped going to meetings. As a result, Republicans now viewed her as a backsliding apostate while Democrats still refused to have anything to do with her, on the not unwarranted assumption that she could still slip money to Republicans out of force of habit.

But widowhood had liberated her. Her driver's license indicated that she was sixty years old (a milestone that somehow slipped by without major notice), but she was a beautiful woman. Silver and light brown hair, cut in a tapered shag, framed her face perfectly. She needed glasses only for reading, and aware of the affect that her brown eyes, almost perpetually sparkling, had on people, she tended to avoid glasses as much as possible. Money had not been a problem, and now that it did not have to be spent on Dr. Don's golf trips, she had plenty to spend on fine clothes and on her hobbies.

Birding fit her lifestyle perfectly. In the summer she still entered short marathons and bicycled hundreds of miles a month. In the winter, she skied—occasionally downhill, but increasingly cross-country. Needless to say, she had organized a local cross country ski club, and had been its first president before she gracefully stepped down "to give others a chance at leadership." As one might imagine, she was in magnificent shape.

The men were in awe of her, and women were jealous or afraid of her, and they all enjoyed each other's company as long as they did what she told them to do. Now, she called on Selma Moen, for her report on the Greater Prairie Chicken.

Selma—taller, plumper, poorer in spirit and pocketbook—had not looked forward to this moment. She felt that she had been talked into giving a lesson on the prairie chicken against her will. She hated speaking in front of crowds, but she could not say no to Carolyn. Without rising from her chair, she said, with somewhat forlorn hope, "Since there are so few here, perhaps we should just forget about my report. We could maybe do it for our next meeting."

"Nonsense," countered Carolyn, "We need to hear it now. By the time we hold our next meeting, the chickens will be booming and the observation blinds will be filling up. Here's what we'll do. You can give us the pleasure of your report, and then I can summarize it and put it on our website."

For Selma, this was getting worse by the moment. Her humble report on a real web site! Web sites were for smart people! She gracelessly got to her feet and shuffled to stand behind a podium. If the truth be known, she tended to look a little like a prairie hen. She wore woven brown slacks, somewhat bulgey, and topped this off with a brown sweatshirt that was appliquéd with patterns of white and rust. She had purchased her little "wearable art" at a craft fair in Detroit Lakes the previous summer, and had been waiting for a chance to wear it. Behind her thick eyeglasses, her small eyes managed to attain a certain amount of beadiness. She spent some time getting her notes together, then tentatively began, "The Greater Prairie Chicken . . ."

At this point, her husband, Earl, rudely exclaimed, "Speak up, Selma, we can barely hear you." In point of fact, everybody but Earl could hear her, but since Earl was deaf as a post, he naturally assumed that everyone else was as well.

Curiously, hearing her "tedious old coot of a husband" spout off made it seem just like home, and she continued with renewed confidence. "The Greater Prairie Chicken—*Tympanuchus cupido pinnatus*—range from Texas to far into Canada. They were once a major game bird and were as numerous as blackbirds. When our ancestors came from Norway, or wherever, if they came from someplace else, they could practically live on the prairie chickens that lived all around their farms. Early pioneer stories told of flocks containing hundreds of birds, but now flocks number less than fifty. In Minnesota, they are now confined to a few scattered grasslands in the western part of the state. But just imagine, before our ancestors, the pioneers, came to take the land from the Indians, all of western Minnesota was an ocean of waving prairie grasses and wild flowers. Sometimes this grass would be over six feet tall, so the people in the covered wagons couldn't even see where they were going. This is what Rolvaag wrote about in *Giants in the Earth,* you know. Well, anyway, these here prairies extended as far as the eye could see, and they were perfect places for prairie chickens."

Selma was pleased to see that her audience was actually paying attention to her. She leaned forward and said: "Again, just imagine, those old pioneers have made it to the prairie and what do they hear? Male prairie chickens, gathering for their almost ritualistic mating dance, would 'boom,' as they call it. The sound has also been described as cooing, tooting, drumming, stamping, cackling, or whooping. Somebody once said it sounded like 'blowing in a conch shell.'

Earl interrupted with: "Who said that?"

"Said what?" countered Selma, annoyed.

"That bit about a conch shell. And what's a conch shell anyhow?"

Selma could have hit him. Instead, she said though clenched teeth, "A conch shell is something you find in the ocean. It's sort of like a gigantic snail shell. And I don't know who said it. I wasn't there. I read it. It is a figure of speech. Satisfied?"

"Okay, okay, don't get huffy, I just wanted to know."

Selma looked back at the rest of the small audience and tried on a smile. "As I was saying, there are only a few areas left in Minnesota where you can find prairie chickens today. Fortunately, some of these areas are very close to Fergus Falls. To the west of here, grasslands have remained on soil considered either too wet or too sandy to support cash crops like corn or soybeans or wheat. This means that farmers left them for a long time as meadows or hayfields and the chickens continued to thrive. However, it remains to be seen how much longer farmers can use these lands for just hayfields or pastures. The habitat, and eventually the survival of the prairie chicken, is in doubt. Indeed, I read that the timber wolf, which is federally protected, is in a far less precarious position in Minnesota than our lovely prairie chicken. In fact," and here Selma paused for effect, "the prairie chicken can be used as an 'indicator species' to tell us the quality of prairie habitats."

As she had hoped, concerned expressions would now find all the faces of her listeners. She continued, "Because a prairie chicken requires large areas of grassland habitat, as long as there are prairie chickens, there will be a prairie. Fortunately, there are those who have taken the initiative to save these beautiful places and these beautiful birds. The Minnesota Department of Natural Resources and the U.S. Fish and Wildlife Service, while not planning specifically for the prairie chicken, have, by taking steps to preserve the native prairie, played an important role in their survival. In addition, about thirty years ago the Nature Conservancy launched a prairie chicken initiative for northwestern Minnesota. Their wonderful actions have resulted in the acquisition of key prairie sites. Unfortunately, however, the number of prairie chickens on private lands continues to decline. There is work for all of us to do!"

As the last six words were escaping her lips, Selma rapidly folded her notes and headed for her seat. She was not, however, fast enough, and Carolyn cut off her path to her chair and said, "I'm sure Selma would be glad to answer any questions you might have."

Selma edged back to the podium, mumbling, "Well, I'm not sure I have much more to say about it." This was the truth. She had said everything she had ever known about prairie chickens, and then some, especially the part about her ancestors eating prairie chickens.

Like a Judas, her own husband, Earl, raised his hand. Grimly, Selma nodded and said, "Earl?"

"Yah, how do you know your ancestors ate those chickens? I never heard anything about that before."

Selma, her own thoughts muddled by thoughts of revenge, replied, "I can certainly understand your not hearing about that before, since I can never recall you showing the slightest interest in my family history. However, while I cannot refer to any family diary that details dining on prairie chickens, I do recall stories about how my ancestors lived off the land. I think it would be safe to assume they ate the chickens. Perhaps *your* folks ate gophers and badgers."

Carolyn quickly jumped in with, "I thought it was a marvelous report, Selma. Where did you get your information?"

"Er, well, I went to the library downtown, and they showed me how to look things up on the Internet. I just typed in 'prairie chicken,' and all that stuff came up."

Earl, not appreciating the crack about the gophers and badgers, came back with, "Most of it? Where did you get the rest?"

This was starting to get uncomfortable. Selma said, "All right, then. I got all of it from the net. Satisfied? In fact, there is a group called the Minnesota Prairie Chicken Society, and, as well as providing me with all of that valuable information, they also provide marvelous tips on viewing the chickens."

Carolyn gave Earl a "time-to-shut-up" look, graciously thanked Selma again, and resumed the podium. With modesty born of confidence, she said "Well, I have been doing a little research myself. I find the prairie chicken to be utterly fascinating, and I think that this year the OTCBWACS should make the prairie chicken our number one focus. In fact, I propose that we have two major priorities. First, we should plan to observe these marvelous birds. As I am sure you all know, Fergus Falls is the southern terminus of the Pine to Prairie Birding Trail and it runs all the way to Warroad on the Lake of the Woods. In this area there are no less than two hundred and seventy-five different species of birds! There are four major areas that the Minnesota DNR and the Fish and Wildlife Service preserved as native prairie habitat. One is east of Crookston, the Glacial Ridge Project, one near Twin Valley that is handicapped accessible, if some of our older members or their friends should require it, one at the Hamden Slough National Wildlife Refuge near Audubon, and, close to home, a project of the Nature Conservancy, is just north of Barnesville.

"Now, these are the major ones, but we don't even have to go that far. The Nature Conservancy also owns an area called the Anna Grunseth Prairie and the Town Hall Prairie, just west of Rothsay, and—even closer to Fergus Falls—we can find the Kettle Drummer Prairie and the Foxholm Prairie, both of which are managed by the Nature Consevancy. These two sites, I am told, represent no less than four hundred and forty acres of alkaline tallgrass. Therefore, I propose that we organize an outing one Saturday in April to observe prairie chickens. What do you think of that?"

A general murmur of consent circled the room.

Satisfied that there was no outward objection to her plan, Carolyn continued, "As to the other matter, I think we should take the 'C' in OTBWACS seriously. I think we should actively work to assist those who are working to preserve the preserve, er, ah, the grasslands for the prairie chickens. How does that sound?"

Everyone listening to her had the same thought. "That sounds like work. Maybe I should quit the organization now. Leave it to that pushy do-gooder to spoil a pleasant pastime like bird watching." But no one had the nerve to do anything but respond with a noncommittal nod.

After a short but uncomfortable silence, Carolyn said, "Anybody? What do you think?"

Ellie Knutson, silent up to now, raised a somewhat chubby hand.

Relieved, Carolyn said, "Yes, Ellie?"

"I think it would be a great idea to go out and observe the chickens. I've never seen a live one. The only one I've seen is that statue in Rothsay, and I have a feeling that they are not really that big." Polite laughter ensued. "Do they look just like that big statue?"

Carolyn, who in fact had also taken all of her information directly off the net, said, " In general, they are about fourteen inches long—about the size of a farm chicken, I suppose. They have a buff plumage barred extensively about the breast, and sometimes darker bars on the back, wings, and belly. The males have a yellow-orange comb over their eyes and dark, elongated head feathers that can be raised along the neck. The most distinguishing thing about the prairie chicken, at least when you're looking at a male, is the circular, orange, unfeathered sac on the neck right below the beak. When the male is in the mood for romance, he inflates this sac. This is what produces that 'booming' noise that they are famous for. The females, like most of the females in the bird kingdom, are considerably more drab—we have male chauvinist pigs, they have male chauvinist roosters—anyway, the females have shorter head feathers and lack the yellow comb and the orange neck sacks."

Stover Stordahl raised his hand. "How come boy boy prairie chickens chickens are prettier than girl girl prairie chickens?"

Carolyn displayed an exaggerated patience with Stover's speech impediment and replied with dripping patronage, "That's just the way it is in nature, um, Stover. You look at the cardinal, for instance. The male is a brilliant red, while the female is rather plain. Or look at the peacock. The male peacock, er, peacock, has brilliant plumage—those magnificent feathers that he loves to show off. The peahen, on the other hand, is really little more than a big chicken. The same goes for prairie chickens."

"But why?" Stover insisted.

With no way out, Carolyn shifted into the mode she had used when she had to teach "candy stripe" volunteers at the local hospital. "You see, it is a part of the male's mating ritual. He wishes to attract a female for purposes of sexual reproduction. If the male prairie chicken shows off his colorful sac and can boom the loudest, a female prairie chicken will be attracted to him. I might go further and say it is really no different than a boy flexing his muscles on the beach to attract a girl."

Stover turned red. He looked at the floor and said, "Yes, I know all that that. But males aren't always the most most colorful." And suddenly Stover was eloquent. "There are a couple of species of phalaropes, which are wading sandpiper-like birds, where the female is much more colorful than the males. It turns out that these female birds court for male attention and, in fact, mate with several males. The males, who are, therefore, not sure whether or not they are the, er, father of the chicks, actually take the lead in egg incubation and chick rearing. This also happens among some tarantulas and some bees. I was just wondering, you know, um, why this didn't happen more often."

Carolyn's self assurance melted as she desperately tried to think of something to say. She had just received a lecture on the birds and the bees! From Stover Stordahl! After several embarassing seconds, she merely said, "I guess I don't know, Stover, but that's an excellent question. Does anybody have an answer to that? No? Well, is there anything else we should discuss?"

"Yah," Selma said, unnecessarily raising her hand. "If we plan on going out to see these birds, I think we should set a date tonight, so that we can plan for it."

"Excellent suggestion," Carolyn responded, "I was about to suggest the same thing myself. What do you have in mind?"

"Well," Selma hesitatingly responded, "according to what I read, April would be a good time, but from what I learned from the website of the Minnesota Prairie Chicken Society, we should make our reservations for a blind as soon as we can, since they are often booked solidly for the weekends. And, since some of our members, especially the ones who are not with us tonight, have to work during the week. I think we should just set a date, reserve the blinds that we need, and go from there. I have a calendar here, with my checkbook, and, well, how does April 15th sound?"

Selma Moen said, "Is that Easter weekend?"

Carolyn looked crossly at her calendar. "Oh yeah, I guess it is. Will this be a problem for anyone?"

Perhaps no one really wanted to make a commitment, but Carolyn took silence as consent and responded. "Great! April 15th it is. Now, I've been looking into this a little bit, and I think this date is ideal. You want to get out there before the grass is green and, preferably, before the frost is completely out of the sod. At this time the greater prairie chickens are, as they say, 'out on their lek.' The 'lek' is the territory that the male chickens defend day after day. They have made it through the challenges of winter, and now they want to do their part to propagate the species with a new brood of chicks. If we plan to see them in their mating ritual, we need to be in place in those blinds well before the crack of dawn. After all, the male prairie chicken has already staked out his territory during the fall and winter, and we will be merely observing those areas that he has chosen for his 'lek.'"

Ellie Knutson interrupted: "You know, both you and Selma keep saying 'male prairie chicken.' Do they ever call 'em roosters?"

"You know, I wondered the same thing. But in all the reading I have done on them, which, perhaps, has not been extensive, I have never come across that term. But that's a good question. Anyway, where was I? Oh, yes, the Minnesota Prairie Chicken Society recommends that we should visit the blind the day before. We will have to find it in the dark, you know, in the morning. Do we have any volunteers to drive either on Friday, for scouting the site, or on Saturday for the viewing?"

Again, Ellie raised her hand and said, "I can go about four o'clock on Friday afternoon, and I'd be glad to give people a ride on Saturday morning."

Earl, who had been mercifully quiet for some time, also acknowledged that he could drive on Saturday.

"Good," said Carolyn, "and I'm sure that some of those who were not able to be here tonight would also be willing to drive. I'm sure I do not have to tell you that mid-April mornings can still be very cold, so you'll need to wear warm clothes. It could even be snowing—this is not a trip for wimps! You'll want to bring along your binoculars and maybe a thermos of coffee.

"So, is it agreed that we can plan that for next month? Now, about the other thing I wanted to bring up. We should also be involved in conservation actions. It has come to my attention that the state of Minnesota actually gave out one hundred and ten permits to hunt prairie chickens in 2005. Does this make any sense to you? Of course not! While we are trying to save them, hunters are trying to kill them with the active connivance of the state. I propose that we do research on the harm this will cause preservation efforts and form a delegation to go to St. Paul and protest. Who would care to join me in this effort?"

Stover Stordahl raised his hand.

"Er, thank you, Stover. Is there anyone else?" Some of the members of her audience actually sat on their hands. "Okay, well, we'll see what some of the others think about this idea. Clearly, we need more bodies for an effective protest. Perhaps I can contact other groups around the state.

"Finally, and I don't know if I should mention this or not, but we could have some good news on the conservation front. Some of you may know Homer Grimstead. Homer is the uncle of Jack Grimstead, who is one of our members who unfortunately seems not to have made it to this meeting. It turns out that Homer Grimstead owns some land just to the southeast of Fergus Falls. It seems that the land isn't good for much by way of agriculture—it's rather sandy and has several sloughs and patches of trees and brush. However, in between all that, there are several small areas of hay fields. He has been leasing out the hay fields for several years but is indicating that he may leave the area to some organization, a group dedicated to the preservation of wildlife, in his will. If he does, well, that is a fine place for the preservation of prairie chickens. I mean, we wish Homer the best of health, of course, but it is a pleasant thought for the, er, distant future.

"So . . . good. Is there any more business? If not, let's just pledge to keep in touch for planning our birding outing for the prairie chickens next month. Meeting adjourned."

As the small group began to struggle into their coats, the tall, distinguished man who had been sitting next to Ellie and who had not spoken a word during the meeting also rose. Ellie brought him up to meet Carolyn. "I'd like you to meet my husband," she said, "Carolyn, this is Palmer Knutson."

"Very glad to meet you," Carolyn said. "Aren't you the sheriff?"

CHAPTER TWO

P ALMER AND ELLIE KNUTSON ZIPPED up their parkas and prepared to face the elements. Just outside the door, Stover Stordahl was greedily pulling on a cigarette which showed about an inch of ember, evidence of the speed in which he sucked it down. Knutson said, "Hey, Stover, do you need a lift?"

Stover smiled politely and replied in a halting stutter, "No thank thank you, Sheriff. Since there wasn't a lot of ice ice on the roads, I rode rode my bike tonight."

"Kind of cold to be riding bike, isn't it?"

"Oh, it's not so bad bad. I got a good good jacket that my mother gave gave me and my rabbit fur fur hat. I can take take it. It's better than walk walking."

"Well if you say so," countered Knutson, secretly glad that he wouldn't have to go out of his way. The Timberwolves were playing Denver, and in spite of his frustration with the team's record, he was looking forward to it. "But you be careful with that thing. I don't think you have enough lights on it."

"Oh, yah, I'll be careful. I always am."

As the Knutsons made their way out to the parking lot, Stover took a final deep drag and carefully deposited the butt into the receptacle. He unlocked his bike and began the mile and a half ride to his apartment. He was not a large man, standing about five feet, eight inches tall and weighing only about one hundred and forty-five pounds. He had rather nondescript reddish brown hair, which was rapidly receding from a sloped forehead. He wore thick-lensed eyeglasses, and his choice of frames had not been a fortunate one. Perhaps it was the smoking that had prematurely aged his face, for he looked far older than his forty-two years.

Stover Stordahl did not have an enemy in the world. Unfortunately, he did not have a friend either. Stover was perhaps the loneliest men in Fergus Falls. Usually, however, he didn't think about this, and had adjusted to the life fate had handed him. He had grown up on a farm near Underwood, the son of single mother who never tried to explain him to anybody. His uncle was one of those bachelor farmers who seem to be found in every rural Minnesota community, and the little family of three had tried to weather the changing nature of modern agriculture. But the surrounding farms got bigger, and Russell Stordahl could not expand, and if he couldn't expand, he couldn't compete. Stover had always assumed he would live on the farm all of his life. He was happy there, far happier than he was in school.

But Russell Stordahl died of a heart attack when Stover was twenty-one, and everybody just knew that

Stover would never be able to take over the farm. His mother, Joyce Stordahl, got a job in a small retirement center on the shores of Battle Lake, and Stover had to leave the only home he had known. The machinery was sold at auction, and the land was sold to a neighbor. Stover's only friend, his dog, was a farm dog that could not be taken to the retirement center, but a neighbor kindly agreed to take care of him. The care lasted a week, or until the dog was run over by Buick station wagon. They said he must have been looking for Stover.

But they didn't call him Stover then, because his name was John. And John Stordahl had not had a happy life. He suffered from Tourette's syndrome, a neuropsychiatric disorder that manifests itself by recurrent muscle tics and involuntary vocalizations. Tourette's syndrome is an inherited disorder that in one form can appear as coprolalia, which is an uncontrollable urge to utter obscene words. No one has yet discovered a cure for Tourette's, but the symptoms do tend to become less severe with age. It has no relevance to the intelligence of the person with the syndrome.

Unfortunately, the severest level of the syndrome is often found during one's teenage years. John, who already felt somewhat of an outsider because of not having a father, had a lonely childhood. When he was born, the local rural church had not exactly gone out of their way to approve of an illegitimate child, and Joyce Stordahl had stopped going to church after John was baptized (somewhat reluctantly by the pastor, Joyce always felt). No Sunday school, no summer socialization. Weeks would go by during which John would never see a child his own age. Yet, these were the happy times. John was not blessed with great intelligence, but he could read and do his numbers. He was not, unfortunately, given any intellectual stimulation at home, and at school his uncontrolled utterances, which he could never understand, embarrassed his fellow students, his teachers, and himself. Kids hear bad words long before they know what they mean. They know they're bad words simply because of how they are used and by the effect they have on other people. John learned the "f-word." At first, they assumed he was a bad boy, and that he must have heard that word all the time at home. Neither assumption was true. One teacher decided he said it all the time just to gain attention, and so she tried to ignore him. Another teacher decided it was a cry for help, and tried to give him extra attention. Most teachers, however, decided it was something "up with which they could not put" and punished him without mercy. It wasn't their fault. They had never heard of Tourette's syndrome, and the presence of someone who would say "that word" three times in quick succession and then act as though he hadn't done a thing, well, you can't let him get by with that.

But there was nothing fundamentally wrong with Stover, and he craved independence from his mother just like any other young man. Although he probably could have operated an automobile safely, he was encouraged by his mother not to do so and totally discouraged by the high school driving instructor. He decided, however, that he wanted to move to Fergus Falls, about as large a city as he had ever known. He discovered that the First Norwegian Lutheran Church of Fergus Falls needed a custodian and decided to apply. Pastor Knutson, the revered head of that particular flock, and older brother of the Otter Tail County sheriff, interviewed him and, although convinced that he could do the job, thought it unseemly for the church janitor to go about his business uncontrollably muttering the "f-word." Still, he did know about Tourette's syndrome, and took pity on the young man. Reverend Knutson reasoned, correctly enough, that college students said the word all the time and that the proper environment for Stover was the athletic complex at Fergus Falls State University. He called in a few favors, and Stover was hired for the only job he would ever hold.

The independent life agreed with Stover. With the help of his mother, he found a small apartment within biking distance of the university, and he did his job well and with pride. He soon became the number one fan of the Fergus Falls Flying Falcons, proudly wearing the school colors to every sporting event. Students noticed him, and began to cheer when he took his usual seat. This pleased him. He had his television, with cable, and he even developed a hobby in bird watching.

It was his second hobby, however, that would provide him with his name. Away from the watchful eye of his mother, he bought a pack of cigarettes. After a few eye-tearing coughs, he discovered he liked it. He tried all brands, filter and non-filter, menthol, lites, short and long, until he finally decided that his ultimate favorite was the first cigarette he had ever tried, Tareyton. There was only one gas station that ever sold that brand, and Stover was probably the only resident of Fergus Falls to appreciate them. He would walk the streets of the town, determinedly poisoning the air around him. It was one of the older residents of Fergus Falls, "Bob the Barber," who remembered the ancient comic strip character of "Smokey Stover." Upon hearing Bob apply the appellation to John, however, others took it up. Over time they dropped the "Smokey" from the name. John didn't like it at first, but, as someone whose whole life had been devoted to adapting to unpleasantness, he accepted it and made it his own. Now, he even signed his name "Stover."

He knew that smoking was "injurious to one's health"—he was told this at least once a day by polite adults and pontificating children—but it was his little way of sticking his thumb in the eye of life. Now he panted as he pedaled his bike through the night air, compulsively counting the number of strokes for each block. Ten strokes from the oak tree and he could coast to the "no parking" sign. Five strokes with the left leg would allow him to coast to the stop sign. He was not sure why he was so obsessed with counting, but a psychologist would have explained it as a manifestation of Tourette's Syndrome. Over the years, he had come to know exactly how many strokes it took to go from his apartment to the Flying Falcon's Field House.

It was a crushingly lonely existence, but he had known no other. When he reached his apartment, he leaned his bike against the back wall and aligned it exactly with a predetermined pattern of bricks. He didn't bother to lock it—no one would ever steal Stover's bike. As he walked in and began to hang up his parka, he smiled. Spring was coming, and he was looking forward to going to the Kettle Drummer Prairie to hear the prairie chickens boom.

Chapter Three

WHEN THE OTTER TAIL COUNTY Bird Watchers and Conservation Society was in the process of adjourning, the March meeting of the Fergus Falls Fin and Feather Club was about to come to order. To be sure, the announced time of the meeting had been the same, but the F.F.F.F. always met in the lower level meeting room of the Veterans of Foreign Wars building. This allowed a few thirsty sportsmen to have a brew before the meeting and allowed others to buy a brew to have with the meeting. Indeed, many of the sportsmen fit into both categories. It allowed for plenty of fellowship in a manner not provided at church choir practice, PTA meetings, or the O.T.C.B.W.C.S.

There were always a lot of stories to tell (or, to be honest, repeat) about fishin', huntin', and Ole and Lena.

". . . so I was pullin' 'em in right and left, you know, but I was really only out there to give my kid a chance. And he wasn't getting a nibble. So I figured I'd even out the odds a bit. I told my kid, I said, 'Look, it's time I let you in on my fishing secret. I'm gonna put on my secret lure.' So I looked into the tackle box for the worst lure I could find, and I seen this here brass button off an old coat that I had years ago. I just slid the hook through the button hole and said, 'Bass can't resist shiny buttons.' I figured if the fish saw only my kid's bait that he would be sure to catch something. Well, sure as hell, I feel this incredible strike. Huge bass! It was three pounds if it was an ounce."

"Did yah eat it or stuff it?"

"Neither. I felt so bad about the kid not getting anything I let it go back in the lake, thinking if he was so damn hungry that he'd bite on a botton, well maybe he would bite on my son's hook. Of course, he never did, and now the kid won't go fishing unless he has a few brass buttons. It's the truth."

"Oh, I believe it. I heard about this one guy who had been putting away a few bottle bass and stood up in the boat to take a whiz and . . ."

Nearby, they were talking hunting and current events. "So, remember when Vice-President Cheyney was out shooting birds and he shot that old guy in the face? What kind of gun did he use?"

"I don't know if they ever said, but it was some kind of shotgun that shoots these tiny little b.b.s—those things get inside your body and stay there."

"I wonder if you can get lead poisoning from them things."

"Nah. They don't use lead anymore. They're made out of steel now."

"Did you hear about when Cheney met up with the Devil? He tells him, 'I can give you anything you want. I can make Halliburton the biggest company the world has yet seen. I can patch up your heart so you'll never have any trouble again. Women? No problem. And you can live to be one hundred and fifty. All I ask in return is your wife's soul, your children's souls, and the souls of your grandchildren and great-grandchildren to rot in hell forever.' So Cheney thought it over and he said, 'So, what's the catch?'"

Some people laughed, some scowled, and some didn't get it at all.

And across the room—"It was the biggest buck I've ever seen. But here I am. I'd just got my deer and I'm dragging it back to the pickup. I was tempted to bury that damn doe in the snow and take that stag. What a rack of antlers! Points? I don't know if I can count that high."

And further across the room—"So this reporter for that big Milwaukee newspaper was driving through Eau Claire, and he looked out of his window just in time to see this huge Doberman pincher attack this seven-year-old boy. Nasty dog—big teeth and drooling out of both sides of his mouth. But just before that dog was about to put his teeth into the kid's throat, another kid, about nine years old, rushed up with a stick. He puts the stick in the dog's collar and gives it a twist and kills the dog and saves the other kid's life. Well, the reporter, he can't believe what he just saw. He rushes up and says, 'That's the greatest act of heroism I've ever witnessed. Kid, I'm gonna make you famous. I'll take your picture and run it with a headline that reads, 'Little

Brewer Fan Saves Life.' What do you think of that?' Well, the kid didn't want to seem ungrateful, but he tells the reporter, "Actually, I'm a Minnesota Twins fan." So, the reporter has another idea. He says, 'I know, I can set up a photo shoot with Aaron Rodgers, and run it with a story line of 'Heroic Packer Meets Heroic Packer Fan!' How about that?' Well, the kid says, "I'm sorry. I'm a Vikings fan.' The next day the headline reads, 'Mean Little Bastard Kills Beloved Family Pet.'"

The joke was well received, and as those who heard it roared in appreciation, it tended to distract the other conversations and the president of the F.F.F.F. Club thought it might be a good time to call the meeting to order. "Shots" Christiansen, who had told the joke and had started telling another, reluctantly stopped after getting only as far as "So Ole and Lena got married, see, and . . ." He looked, with a certain amount of resentment, to Roger Foss who, with practiced eloquence, said, "All right, all right, all right. Everybody here who's going to be here? If you're not here, speak up! (The kids in sixth grade said the pledge of allegiance with less regularity than Foss used that gag.) Then maybe we should start? Anybody got a secretary's report? Who was supposed to take minutes of the meeting last month?"

Pete Hanson said, "well, I remember we talked about that, because we had to elect somebody because Garth Herzog, who used to do it, was being put in the old folks home by his son, but I don't think we got as far as getting someone else to do it."

"All right, then," Foss resumed, trying to maintain control, "anybody remember what we talked about?"

Jim Lomsdahl said, "All I can remember is Shots bitching about the Vikings, and somebody said something about prairie chickens."

"That's right," Foss said, "we were going to talk about prairie chickens," Foss nodded in a challenge to anyone who had anything to add. He was a take-charge leader, a high school athlete for the Fergus Falls Otters who still had his letter jacket. He wore a crew cut, the same hair fashion he had when he showed up at his first University of Minnesota Football practice in the fall of 1962. It did not take long for him to realize that Big Ten athletes had a different level of size and speed than he had. After forty minutes of calisthenics, he "hurt his knee," turned in his pads, and spent the rest of his life telling people how much he wanted to compete at the university level, but that fate had decreed otherwise. He returned to take a job at the lumberyard, and became the star of the town softball team for the next thirty-five years and gave himself the nickname of "the Chief." Over the years, his belt had gotten longer, but he still acted as though he could play if he wanted to play. He was just about to tell everyone what he knew about prairie chickens, when Dickie Clark unexpectedly stood up.

Nobody called him Dick Clark. To confuse him with the cool and ageless rock and roll icon would have been impossible. Dickie was aging ungracefully, with wispy hair combed over a dented skull and shirt buttons that were losing the fight against his expanding belly. "The Chief" had once unkindly accused him of having "Dunlop's syndrome,"—"Yer belly's done lopped over your belt"—and it was all too true. Now he shyly said, "Well, Chief, you told us all to find out something about the prairie chickens, so I figured you meant me, so I prepared a little report."

Needless to say, everyone was stunned. Nobody ever gave a report to the F.F.F. F. Club! But Chief at least had the presence of mind to welcome such a development and said, "Well, then, Dickie, let's hear it."

Dickie laboriously puffed to the front of the room, fished out oversized black reading glasses, hitched up his pants, wiped drool from his lower lip, and wheezed: "Well, what I have here is something I got off the Internet. It is a report from Michael A. Larson, a grouse research biologist, from the Forest Wildlife and Research Group up in Grand Rapids."

Jaws dropped throughout the audience. Dickie had a computer? And he knew how to use it? Was that possible?

Breaking the silence with his reedy voice, Dickie said, "As you may know, there was no hunting season for prairie chickens—the proper name for which is *tympanuchus cupido pinnatus* (To give him credit, Dickie pronounced this with a reasonable degree of accuracy, but the crowd groaned nevertheless.)—from 1943 until 2002. Think of it! In 2003 there was hardly a person in the whole county who had ever shot, legally at least, a prairie chicken. I don't know if my grandfather ever shot one before he went off to World War II, but he couldn't shoot one afterwards. But, in October of 2003 a limited five day hunting season for prairie chickens was held within seven permit areas in western Minnesota. These hunting permits were awarded on a lottery basis, and each hunter could take a maximum of two chickens— or 'harvest' the prairie chickens, as the report says. This seemed to work so well that five day seasons were also held in 2004 and 2005.

"Now, the thing is, as we know, a grouse looks a hell of a lot like a prairie chicken when you're walking through the grass or the stubble of a field. The prairie chicken permit areas were established in places where you weren't supposed to shoot a grouse, which, by the way, around here, anyhow, is the sharp-tailed grouse— the *T. phasianellus campestris*—(more groans) and apparently, a few hunters blasted them even if they weren't supposed to. So, last year they changed the law to allow all those guys who had the prairie chicken permit, who were also licensed to hunt grouse, to shoot 'em both at the same time, er, I mean, shoot them both in the same place, I mean, in the same field in the same day. Well, you know what I mean. Before, you almost had to shoot 'em both and then hold them up to see the difference. Now you can just blast away."

A voice from the back of the room snidely inferred that if wouldn't make any difference to Dickie, since he couldn't hit anything anyway. Dickie ignored this and went on. "This report that I read said that there were one hundred and ten permits available for 2005, and that nineteen percent of the 487 regular applicants got a permit. Now, you might find this interesting, there were 835 applicants in 2003 and 734 in 2004. I don't know if people got discouraged or what, but it looks like the chance of getting a permit to hunt prairie chickens is getting better all the time. And, get this, according to this here report, sixty percent of the hunters reported getting, er, harvesting, a prairie chicken. And eighteen percent of the hunters reported that they also flushed out sharp-tailed grouse. Apparently those hunters who were lucky enough to get permits liked it so much that eighty-eight percent of 'em said they were going to apply again this year.

"And finally, you know where the best hunting was? Right in our own backyard. It's the area just west of the interstate between here and Barnesville. Boys, I say, let's go hunt some prairie chickens."

Someone clapped his hands, and another joined him. Soon the whole club was applauding Dickie Clark for the first time in his life. He shyly nodded his appreciation. Chief joined in the clapping as he moved in beside Dickie and nudged him back toward his seat. Hoping to regain the center of attention, he said, "Good job, Dickie, good job. So, that it boys? Anybody got any new business?"

"Yah," said Danny Kittleson, " what kind of gun do you use for prairie chickens?"

Chief had been looking for an opportunity to brag about his gun all night long. "Well, I tell you boys, I just got me a new twenty-gauge Remington 870 pump, and I'm looking forward to trying it out."

"What size shot you planning on usin'?" came a question from the rear.

"Oh, I figure my new gun should handle number five or number six pretty well."

"Is that the size of the pellets that Cheney used to shoot that guy in the face?"

"How would I know? I think they use real small ones for that. Anybody got anything else to say?"

Emboldened by Dickie's report, Shots Christiansen stood up to voice a concern that had been building up for some months. Shots had received some unasked for address stickers from a Sierra Club membership drive. He loved the animals on the stickers, and he was pleasantly surprised that someone had actually spelled his last name correctly ("It's 'e-n'—I'm a Dane, you know.") and had used his baptismal name of John. He had never liked the name "Shots," since it referred to that time twenty-two years ago when he had been hunting pheasants and the neighbor's dog jumped up in the grass and he shot him right in the head. He felt bad about that, but he felt even worse when everyone teased him about it. The owner of the dog demanded a hundred bucks from Shots, and then bragged that he had been planning to shoot the dog himself the next week. Now, he even felt a certain amount of solidarity with Vice-President Cheney. In any event, he felt guilty using the address labels without paying for them, and so he had sent a check to the Sierra Club. He even started to read their literature. He had a solid opinion at last!

"Yah," he bravely said, "I got something. We always talk about us being a conservation society, but we never do anything except shoot animals, lie about fishing, hold game feeds, and generally b.s. about things. I think we should do something positive in the way of conservation."

Surprisingly, Chief looked at him and said, "Good point, 'Shots,' I've been thinking the same thing myself." He looked over to old Homer Grimstead and said, "Homer, can I tell them what you were telling me about your plans?"

Homer, who had no intention of talking about his plans, was clearly in a bind. To clam up now that Chief had started to let the cat out of the bag would seem to be overly secretive. He stood up and said, "Nei, I tink I'll yust tell everybody myself, but don't spread dis around, yew know, cus I ain't got it vorked out yet."

He ambled up to the front of the room while adjusting his pants and the buttons of his cardigan sweater vest, which rather clashed with the Vikings sweatshirt he was wearing underneath the vest. Homer didn't hunt anymore, a fact that was appreciated by Otter Tail County residents and pets alike, but he still loved to fish. He also liked beer, a factor in his never missing a meeting of the F.F.F.F. Club. As he turned around to speak, Chief thought to himself, "I remember him when he was ten inches taller."

"Vell, yew see," he began in a somewhat shaky voice, "I vas yust telling Chief here about my eighty acres down sout of here along da interstate. It ain't never been good for much. It's yust a bunch of sloughs and some trees and a little hay land. Vell, I been renting out da hay land ever since I quit farming myself. I sold da good stuff. Dat and Social Security is vat I yoose to buy my beer." (This was accompanied with a wheezing laugh and was appreciated by all.) So, anyhow, I get a little rent from it, but den I gotta pay taxes on it tew, you know. It ain't wort all dat much. So I got to tinking, maybe I should yust give dat land away. Yuse guys been talking about shooting dose prairie shickens and dere are a lot of dem dere, and I know a lot of yuse been hunting deer dere, tew. Vell, dat's all right, dat's about da only ting dat it's good for.

"But, as some of yuse may have noticed, I ain't getting any younger." This statement was followed by a chorus of denials. "So, anyvay, I vas telling Chief here dat I vas tinking of leaving it all to yuse guys in my vill. Dat vay, nobody is going to come along and drain da sloughs and start farming it. Ting is, I don't know how to do dat. As Chief told me, dis club ain't, vat yew call it, Chief, 'incorporated.' Vell, I don't know about dat, but maybe I'll look into giving it to dat 'Nature Conservancy' dat we hear about, or maybe give it to da state of Minnesota— dey ought to be able to figger out someting for me. Or, who knows? Maybe yuse guys can get yerselfs 'corporated.' But if I do dis, yuse guys gotta promise me dat every time you shoot vun of dem dere shickens, you'll tink of me. But don't start tinking about dat too much, cus I'm still above ground and expect to stay dat vay."

Chief stood up and slapped him on the back with enough force to alter Homer's just expressed opinion. "What do you say, boys, how about that Homer!" Applause broke out to the extent that it exceeded the previous club record which had been set only moments before. "Homer," Chief shouted, "let me be the first to buy you a beer! Let's adjourn this meeting and go upstairs." For this motion, opposed by no one, there was no need for a formal vote.

Chapter Four

PALMER KNUTSON UTTERED A MILD expletive under his breath and began searching for the remote. The Minnesota Timberwolves had let him down again. At least this time he did not have to suffer through a late-game collapse, since they had lately perfected the second quarter collapse. *Why do I waste my time watching those clowns?* he thought, not for the first time. With a sigh of exasperation, he realized that the remote had slipped down under the cushions of his blue leather chair, which had been known, for some time now, as "Dad's chair." He was almost forced to take the chair apart before he found it, and his resolve to go right up to bed had faded. Ellie had gone upstairs long ago to watch *The Daily Show* and enjoy Jon Stewart skewer yet another right-wing wind bag. She had probably fallen asleep by this time anyhow.

He mindlessly surfed the channels. *Is this why I'm paying forty-seven bucks a month to that cable company? Eighty channels and nothing to watch! How many times are they going to show Brendan Frazier battle that damned mummy?* He would have turned off the television long ago, but he dreaded the fourteen-step climb to the bedroom.

It was not that he was in bad shape. In fact, the observation had often been made that he was in "good shape." Unfortunately it was always accompanied by "for a man of your age." He still shot baskets in the driveway with his son, he tried to walk more than he had to, and he made sporadic attempts to discipline his life to the demands of a Nordic Trak exercise unit that perpetually mocked him. Once the youngest elected sheriff in the state of MInnesota, he was now referred to, as often as not, as "good old Palmer" and heard increasingly familiar stories from people who said, "Yeah, our son was telling us that you visited his social studies class, just like you visited our class when I was in high school." He'd had thicker hair then, and there had been no gray. He had looked trim and dashing in his sheriff's uniform. These situations no longer existed. He pressed the remote and turned on the DVD player. This provoked another mild whispered oath. He found his bifocals and was able to turn everything off.

He looked forward to bed. It was the ultimate refuge, especially since he and Ellie had acquired a thick queen size down comforter made in Austria. It had been a twenty-fifth wedding anniversary gift from their three children. Talk about a gift that keeps on giving! Palmer appreciated it ever so much more than a silver tea set.

To his surprise, Ellie was still awake, watching *Letterman*. It was a repeat, but since Ellie had slept through it the first time, it was new to her. He joined her in bed and when Letterman introduced a new rap sensation, they quickly turned it off. "Rap musician! The ultimate oxymoron! So, how did the Woofies do?" she asked. Palmer let loose a suffering wheeze and answered, "They lost, as usual."

"Why do you waste your time watching those clowns?" Since it was still March, Ellie was wearing her flannel nightgown, which Palmer appreciated as being "cuddly." She wore her hair in a no-longer-fashionable shag, and now, as she removed her oversized glasses, Palmer gazed at the blue eyes with which he had fallen in love almost forty years ago. She considered herself a little too plump, and definitely too old, but Palmer thought she was the most beautiful woman in the world.

"I dunno," Palmer said as he fluffed up his pillow and took an Ian Rankin novel off of the night stand, "I should have been reading my book. The thing I like about these Rankin books is the setting. Modern day Edinburgh. I'd love to go there one day, although sometimes he makes it seem like a tough town—not as tough as Glasgow, of course—but a tough place for law enforcement. It makes me glad I live in Otter Tail County. This Edinburgh inspector is always in some kind of danger. The only time I'm threatened is on election day."

"That reminds me, Palmer, um, this is an election year. You haven't even told me whether or not you plan to run again. And don't you have to file for election pretty soon?"

"That's right, I suppose I do. I knew there was something. I thought it was time to renew my driver's license. Actually, though, I don't think the filing deadline is until sometime at the end of June . . . or something . . . I'll look it up. But, yah, I suppose I will. I mean, it's not like I have anything else to do. I guess I just sort of figured that at this time next year I would still be sheriff . . . um . . . what do you think?"

"Well, I'm glad you asked me for my opinion. First, as a wife, I want you to be happy with your job. If you hated it, I'd tell you to quit. Your pension must be doing all right, in spite of the horrible economy we inherited from the 'Bushies.' If you wanted to quit, I'd support your decision all the way. But you seem to like what you do so, if you're happy, I'm happy. But second, as a citizen, I can tell you that this county has never been served as well, nor will it be served as well in the future, than it has been by our present sheriff. I mean that. I hear it almost every day ,and it makes me very proud. Do you think anybody would be foolish enough to run against you?"

"Oh, probably not. I haven't heard of any overly ambitious constables. I think Orly Peterson would like my job some day, though. And he'd do all right, too. The only thing is, as you know, my position is nonpartisan, and a few of the people in the county think I'm married to a left-wing loony. I suppose if they can, in the end, hold their nose and vote for me under those conditions, I might be reelected."

"But you know," Ellie said in a serious tone, "that's something we should think about—retirement, I mean. You don't want to end up like one those Old West sheriffs who get so slow on the draw they become the target of every young gunslinger in the territory. Imagine the humiliation of getting called out on Lincoln Avenue and not being able to strap on your shootin' iron because of your arthritis! But seriously, if you quit, I quit. Then we have to think about whether or not we still want to live in Fergus Falls. Other than your brother, we really don't have much family here anymore. The girls have already gone, and once Trygve finishes college, I don't suppose he'll come back here to live. Some people move south. Think you'd like to do that?

"No. I was born a Minnesotan, and I'll die a Minnesotan. I like the seasons, the land, and the people, and, besides, I don't want to go somewhere where I can't turn on the television and watch the Twins and Vikings. I even suffer along with the Gophers. Still, I'd like the freedom to pick up and go somewhere whenever I felt like it. I'd like to go to Edinburgh, for instance."

"Think they need your help?"

"Well, they might. I've solved a lot cases fifty pages before the end," Palmer said, a clear indication that, although he enjoyed the chat, he would prefer to get in just a few pages before he fell into the arms of Morpheus. He repuffed his pillow.

But Ellie was wide awake, and wanted to talk more. "You know, we could do something completely different. Did you know that Nora's Knitting Nook might be closing? I was just in there today, and Nora seemed so depressed. She told me that she wanted to quit a long time ago, but that there was no place else that sold the yarns she did and that she didn't want to let people down and so she stayed open, as she said, sort of as a favor to everybody, and I told her that that was no way to run a business and she said that if she had her way she would close the door tomorrow but that she still had quite a bit of inventory left and she figured she would just keep it up but when she thought about ordering new yarns, and she said there was so much new stuff, like Icelandic woolens and new stuff from the orient, that she just got tired trying to keep track of it. So anyway, that's the sort of thing that we could do. We could retire and then run a small business, like Nora's Knitting Nook. I think we would be good at that, don't you?"

Palmer was losing patience. "Moomph, maybe, but what part of the word 'retire' don't you understand. Sure, we could do that—get up early every morning and open a store—or we could live modestly off of my pension and, don't forget, that lavish Social Security check, and then go off to Edinburgh whenever we wanted to. Maybe in the fall. The plane tickets are far cheaper then, and there aren't so many tourists and the weather in Scotland is still nice in September. We could rent a car and drive around the Highlands and maybe even go over to the Isle of Skye. We could stay in a little B and B in Inverness and then go out and look for the

Loch Ness Monster. We could vanish in the mists of Brigadoon. We could buy you a little kilt. How does that sound?"

"Sounds good. Buy why stop at just getting a kilt for me. You would look cute in a kilt yourself. What would you wear under it?"

"Well, that's the eternal question, isn't it?"

"So, you have been giving some thought to retirement, after all!"

"Well, maybe just a little," Palmer conceded.

Palmer picked up his Rankin novel while Ellie turned away and within a remarkably short time was sound asleep. But the sheriff found it hard to concentrate. Maybe he should quit the whole law enforcement scene. It was no longer as pleasant as it used to be. And really, how much money in the retirement kitty did he need? For years he and Ellie, who worked as a social worker for Otter Tail County, had been salting away extra 401K benefits. The pension fund was recovering a little bit. It wouldn't be long before Trygve was done with St. Olaf College, so that would be the last of the tuition expenses. And then what? His daughter Maj, who had graduated from Gustavus Adolphus College in St. Peter, Minnesota, had a nice job teaching at a middle school in a Minneapolis suburb (an eighth grade teacher, a short cut to canonization as a saint). His second daughter, Amy, had graduated from Concordia College in Moorhead and was now in her second year of law school. Neither of them were likely to come back to Fergus Falls to live. No, if they wanted to be near their children, they would have to move near to where they were and not vice-versa. So then where? Red Wing was nice, so was Northfield, and, of course, Rochester, where he would be close to the Mayo Clinic for his final days. "No," he thought, "I'm becoming morbid. But if we lived in Northfield, we would be only about thirty miles from the Minneapolis airport and we could leave at a moment's notice and hop on a plane to Edinburgh and help John Rebus solve this murder and . . ." Zzzz.

CHAPTER FIVE

THE FOLLOWING MONDAY, CONGRESSMAN Glenn Paulson appeared at a special press conference to announce the formation of the Western Minnesota Farmers Energy Cooperative. This organization was a result of years of united efforts by the Minnesota Farmers Union, "Green" organizations, civic organizations, and the creative efforts of bankers and investors throughout Minnesota. It was the perfect opportunity, therefore, for Congressman Paulson to claim full credit.

The conference was held at the Hubert H. Humphrey Room at the Fergus Falls State University Student Union. Academic sites were generally avoided by the congressman, since he perceived, correctly, a deep animosity towards him by academics.

This was well earned. The congressman represented everything that was wrong with American politics. He had ridden to office as a progressive, eager to wipe out the cronyism that had infected the last few years of his predecessor. He soon discovered that cronyism was an ideology to his own liking. To be sure, he still appeared to hang around a few county fairs near election time, but since his district covered more than a quarter of the state and was relatively sparsely populated, voters often gave him the benefit of a doubt and just assumed that he was helping some other poor farmer. In fact, he usually wasn't, and he had grown to loathe them.

He was, however, unbeatable. Such were the advantages of incumbency that he would never fear a serious challenge from his own Democratic party, and most Republicans had nothing to gain from unseating him. A "Blue Dog" democrat, he supported the Republicans on virtually everything, including a bill to cut inheritance taxes for all those who made more than five million dollars. But it was not this vote that created for him a determined enemy by the name of Ellie Knutson. Ellie was on the board of the local Planned Parenthood. Paulson's slavish kowtowing to extremist elements who did everything they could to sabatoge the merest hint of birth control information had made him the ultimate enemy in the eyes of Ellie.

As the sheriff was getting dressed on that Monday morning, Ellie said, "My, don't you look spiffy! What's the occasion for the full uniform?"

"Ah, it's one of those 'show the flag' events. Glenn Paulson is coming to the university to announce the construction of that big ethanol plant that people have been talking about for several years. All the other elected officials are going to be there, from the state representatives to Mayor Armbruster. I thought I'd look like kind of a dog in the manger if I didn't show up. Um," he said, hopefully, "I don't suppose you're going to go to the press conference today, are you?"

Ellie put her face within two inches of Palmer's nose and said, "You bet I'm going to go. I want to grill that S.O.B. on every betrayal he has made to our party. See if I don't!"

Palmer could tell that he would not be leaving for his office very soon. He sat down on the bed. He tried to sound the very voice of reason as he said, "Yes, but you see, it's a press conference. That means the media —TV reporters, newspaper people—those are the only ones who get to ask the questions. Since he knows you, and fears you, I might add, it is unlikely that he'll be fooled into calling on you."

"But someone has to expose what he's doing. Do you know he was one of the few Democrats to support every single one of Bush's tax cut for the rich? I mean, a person who makes $20,000 to $30,000 a year gets a tax cut of ten bucks. Ten bucks! Some yokel in a trailer house votes for him for the ten bucks. The guy who makes a million gets his taxes cut by $42,500! This guy calls himself a Democrat?"

"Well," Palmer said lamely, "I suppose the guy who got the ten bucks would say that he could buy a pizza . . ."

"My point exactly," Ellie interrupted, "those people sell their soul for a pizza! And how can we get rid of him.

He supports every loony right-wing idea. Women's rights? He's against them. Stem cell research? He's against it for moral reasons—as if he ever made a moral decision in his life. Guns? If the National Rifle Organization, which generously fills his campaign coffers, wanted to protect the manufacture and sale of guns that were specially designed to allow high school kids to shoot their teachers, he would be all for it. So all the poor Republicans can do is find some poor sap who claims that Paulson is a flaming liberal and he must be replaced with someone who thinks the Nazis were a bunch of sissies. I tell you, Jefferson is spinning in his grave! That man is just lower than . . . lower than . . . lower than whale poop!"

Palmer smiled both at the illusion and his wife's delicacy, then countered: "Hey, be fair to the man. He has a logical policy for guns. If the high school kid gets a gun to shoot his teacher, he would say that the only logical thing to do would be to give the teacher a bigger gun. This kind of Mexican standoff would ultimately produce peace through mutual deterence. Moreover, it would be good for the economy, as every gun manufacturer would be rolling in dough from selling anti-student personel weapons." Years ago, Palmer was concerned that Ellie's passion for social justice might count against him in the general election. He knew better than to try to silence her, however, and as he grew more confident in his job, he enjoyed her passion and wished that he could be more like her. Even though he had come to share her sentiments, however, he was too much of a stoical Norwegian to be as vocal. "But you know, um, you could find a ringer. You might be able to get Stacie Ryan, the *Daily Journal* reporter, to ask your questions for you. She's often ready to stir a few things up."

"That's a good idea," Ellie relented, "I'm going to call her right now."

After a few moments, Ellie joined him at the breakfast table with a sly grin on her face. "What did you find out?" her husband asked.

"Well, she didn't say she would, but she didn't say she wouldn't. I'm going to meet her at eleven o'clock and we'll talk about it. But if she doesn't, I'm just going to have to do it myself."

Palmer finished his breakfast as he dreaded the possibilities. As Ellie grabbed a legal pad and furiously began writing, he saw this as a good opportunity to slip out. He gave a her a hasty peck on the mouth and was soon out the door on the way to his garage and his beloved black Acura TL 3.2. He had driven an Acura Integra for several years, worrying about how the local voters would accept their sheriff in a foreign car, since he was provided with a car allowance by the county. But they accepted it, and when it needed to be replaced at last, he had splurged and bought the TL—"The Limo"— leather seats, power everything, and an incomparable Bose sound system. Ah, life was good.

T HREE HOURS LATER, at the press conference, Congressman Paulson stood before the movers and shakers of western Minnesota. He had decided to take a folksy approach, and had eschewed his Pierre Cardin suit for an open jeans jacket. His puffy belly, enhanced by lobbiest Scotch and steak dinners, strained against a belt held together by a steer's head buckle. He proceeded to laud the work done by himself and everyone on his staff to bring about the tremendous opportunities that lay before the Western Minnesota Farmers Energy Cooperative. To polite applause, he called upon Aldwin Monson, the president of the organization—and, as head of First Federal of Fergus Falls, a major lender—to describe the project.

Monson, wearing as fine a suit as had ever been seen in several states, beamed at the audience and began, "It is my distinct pleasure to announce to you that we are in the final stages of completing the details for the construction of an eighty-million-dollar ethanol plant to be built right here in Otter Tail County. Most of the materials will be purchased locally, most of the construction labor force will be from around here, and, of course, the raw materials for the production of energy—clean, efficient domestically produced energy— will be grown here. Ladies and gentlemen, we are on the edge of an ethanol revolution. A pure source of energy that's renewable and will liberate us from dependence on foreign oil. I'm sure all of you are aware of the high cost of gasoline when you fill up at our local filling stations. Remember, it is not our local merchants that are getting rich off of all that—no, it is a bunch of crazy Arabs who hate our guts. I look out at you today, and think about how our dreams have come together, and think that this is the most patriotic thing I have ever done. And . . ."

This rhetoric went on, in painful hyperbole, for another twenty minutes.

"So I thank Congressman Paulson for all that he has done (*which is damn little*, he thought) and recognize all those who have been doing committee work for so long to create this organization. Now, if there are any questions, I'm sure that the Congressman and I will do our best to answer them."

A reporter for WDAY television in Fargo raised his hand and lobbed a softball: "When do you think you will be able to break ground for the new plant?"

Monson politely looked to Paulson, knowing full well he knew nothing about the project, and then said, "Actually, we have the financing all lined up. We have yet to select a site, however, but we do have a few places in mind. If we can find the right place, we'll have to do an environmental study, and then, I don't know, I would think we could start on it yet this summer."

Another reporter asked, "What are you looking for in a site?"

This time, Monson did not bother to make eye contact with Paulson and said, "Well, I think the most important consideration is transportation. We need to be near the railroad tracks, so we can build a spur off of that. And we would also like to be near the interstate. A lot of our finished product will be shipped by truck, of course, and besides, we need to have a good system of roads to get the corn to the ethanol plant. Although the odor from a modern ethanol plant is practically nonexistent, or so I'm told, we do not want it to be in a town. On the other hand, we want to be close enough to a residential area so that our workers do not face a hardship commuting to work. We have already identified two or three areas that would suit our needs. Are there any more questions?"

Sheriff Knutson, seated near the front cringed and held his breath. He had seen his wife in the back of the room, but had studiously avoided eye contact. This could be her time to shine.

But Stacie Ryan, taking a quick look at her note card, stood and said, "I have a question for Congressman Paulson. Haven't you, sir, in the past, been quite negative about the possibilities inherent in ethanol? I notice by your voting record that you have consistently voted on the side of "big oil" and said, less than a year ago, if I may quote, 'that ethanol stuff isn't going to work. It takes more gas to produce it than it saves. We ought to just drill for more oil. We got plenty of it in Alaska.' You seem to have changed your mind."

With a disdainful sneer, Paulson muttered, "I never said that."

Ryan cheerfully pointed out, "Perhaps not, but you were quoted as saying exactly that in *Newsweek* and in the *Minneapolis StarTribune*. These were remarks made to the Upper Midwest Petroleum Council on May 16th of last year. It does seem that you have indeed changed your mind, Congressman."

"I'm sure that was taken out of context. I believe I was responding to the issue of whether or not we could make ethanol out of sugar beets. I still consider that to be a misuse of resources. The sugar manufacturers support me on this. Next question."

Unfortunately, none of the other reporters was anxious to be recognized, and Ryan continued, "Yes, I suspect 'big sugar' would say that, and, as we are all aware, 'big sugar' is one of the most generous of all donors to your campaigns, but as you no doubt know, Brazil produces virtually all of its energy needs from ethanol made from sugar cane. They don't even need to buy oil from Venezuela, let alone Iran."

The sheriff could no longer resist. He craned his neck to look back at his wife. She was beaming and, seeing her husband's look, gave him a conspiratorial wink.

A long pause ensued while Paulson glared at the reporter with the distain he usually reserved for lite beer. Finally, a reporter from the *Fargo Forum*, long a faithful supporter of the congressman, said, "How committed is this plant to the production of ethanol from corn. Have you considered other sources?"

Monson, eager to move on from the air of confrontation pervading the room, stepped up and said, "Yes, of course we have. Corn, in its kernel form, is the most viable crop for ethanol production right now. But we project a time in the near future when it'll be possible to use the entire plant, including the stalk. Furthermore, if it proves out that switch grass or some other renewable resource is more efficient, we'll be able to convert this plant to that. In fact, recent studies by the University of Minnesota indicate that a wide mixture of grasses, that can grow in almost any type of soil, may be the most useful for producing energy. The most important thing is that the farmers of western Minnesota will have a ready market for their crops and the project will benefit the entire region. And, as I say, as soon as we have a site available, we can go into production."

There were a few more technical questions as to the number of workers that would be utilized in construction of the plant and how many would be employed when full production began and whether or not they would be unionized. Monson deftly fielded all questions, including potential odors associated with production. Finally, he said, "Congressman, is there anything else you'd like to add?"

Paulson stood, somewhat nervous but, reassured that the snotty reporter was not about to ask another question, turned to the audience and beamed. "Yes, as I am sure you all know, I've opened a district office in the Kaddatz building right here in Fergus Falls." Most of the members of the audience looked somewhat bewildered. This was news to them. In fact, the congressman had decided to keep the office underpublicized, on the theory that the less people knew about it, the less they would take advantage of the situation to propose that he do some actual constituent work. He continued: "This will enable my staff to keep a close watch on this great project, and we'll be able to facilitate both the construction and initial phases of production of the ethanol. I'd like to introduce, at this time, my administrative assistant. His name is Chadd Hangar, and he'll be my point man here in Fergus Falls. Chadd, stand up so the people can see what you look like."

A rather pudgy short young man in a three-piece suit stood and rather furtively nodded to the right and the left and then sat down. There was mild applause. With this, the congressman abruptly began to stride for the exit, a clear announcement that the conference was over. He was immediately joined at the door by Chadd Hangar and was overheard to whisper, "Make sure you take care of things so I don't have to come back to Fergus Falls for another couple of years."

Chapter Six

THERE WAS ONE OTHER meeting of significance that day. Homer Grimstead had telephoned his nephew Jack and asked that he accompany him to the First Federal of Fergus Falls bank for a meeting "dat vill truly be in yer interest." Jack agreed to accompany him, but as in all his relationships with his uncle, he looked forward to it as he would a root canal. He was standing outside of his seedy duplex, huddling against the March wind, when Homer drove up in his old Cadillac Fleetwood. As he opened the door to get in, Homer grunted, "How come yer standing out dere in da cold? I could'a come in and got yew, yew know."

Jack, who wanted to prevent this very thing in the event that his uncle would try to make himself at home amongst his beer bottles and pizza cartons, put the best face on things by saying, "No, no, I just wanted to save you the trouble."

They rode together in uneasy silence down the middle of the street at a speed that would not have been admired by a crippled turtle. At times, Homer slammed on his brakes, apparently anticipating that a parked or unoccupied van would suddenly become animated and lurch out at him. Finally, Jack could take it no longer and asked, "So, what's this all about then."

Homer chuckled and said, "Jack, my boy," (the thirty-eight-year-old nephew winced) "yew are my only living relative. I'm not getting any younger, and I got to tink about vhat vill happen ven I'm gone. I made my vill out a long time ago, and I'm leaving almost everyting I got to yew. Dis car, fer instance, vill vun day be yers."

Oh, good, thought Jack. *Just what I have always wanted! A sixteen-year-old Cadillac that gets nine miles to the gallon! At least it has a cassette player instead of an eight track.*

A mailbox escaped to stand another day by the slimmest of margins, and Homer went on, "But yew know, dere are yust a couple of otter tings I wanted to take care of, so I asked my old friend at da bank, Aldwin Monson, to meet vit us dis afternoon. Yew know, I wished yew had kept dat yob in da bank. Dat vas a good yob, vit plenty of room fer advancement. Yew should'a stayed dere."

Oh,God, this again, thought Jack. *What did I tell him last time? I can hardly tell him that "Good old Aldwin" allowed me to resign and agreed not to press charges when he caught me palming that C-note out of the cash drawer.* Aloud he said, "At the time, I just thought I had a better future in real estate."

"But dat ain't vorked out so good, has it? Yew know, yew might have been better off to connect vit one of dem big real estate companies radder den going independent."

Jack hated it when his uncle was right—it had been a dumb thing to do. How many of life's foibles could be explained with a nimble "It seemed like a good idea at the time?" He had studied for and passed his realtor's examination and had been able to lease a ground floor office in the restored historic Kaddatz Hotel for a pittance because the developer wanted to brag that it was fully utilized and successful. In truth, his office had once been the first floor linen closet. It had room for a desk, a filing cabinet, and two chairs for potential clients. At first, business had been fairly steady, and he made enough to eat and pay his phone bill, but pretty soon it was apparent that the real money was to be had in buying and selling lake property. Anybody who had lake property to sell learned pretty quickly that the big real estate companies, with all their websites, could offer a lot better service than he could. It had been a bad couple of years. Jack was not in the mood for having his past dissected and his future planned by an old fool, and muttered, "Well, I think things will be turning around soon." He turned to stare out of the window to indicate that he no longer wanted to discuss the issue.

Homer guided his Cadillac into the parking lot of the First Federal of Fergus Falls and neatly aligned the hood ornament with the center of the yellow lane marker. Jack wanted to dash into the bank to stay warm, but politeness won out and he stayed with his uncle for the duration of a walk which rivaled the time Amundsen needed to trek to the South Pole.

* *

ALDWIN MONSON WAS WAITING FOR THEM. He ushered them into his office and offered coffee from a chrome carafe. "Yew bet," Homer said, "I never turned down a cup of coffee in my life." Jack, understandably uncomfortable in the presence of his former employer, declined.

Monson was in a perky mood. "Well, you came on a good day. Today is one of the best days of my life. As you may have heard, we had a big do up at the University today. The congressman was there and everything. I've got a lot to celebrate—maybe I should be serving brandy and cigars instead of coffee."

Jack ruefully observed that he was only kidding.

"See," Monson went on, "I've been working for over a year to put together the financing for the new ethanol plant. That's my baby. I mean, I'm not going to run it or anything—my part is essentially done—but they couldn't have done it without me. And it has really raised the profile of the bank. In fact," and Monson lapsed into a long hesitation during which time he appeared to exert every effort to hold his tongue, "well, maybe I shouldn't show you this. Hardly anybody has seen it before, but you're an old friend, Homer, and I know I can trust you." Monson whipped out a set of computer enhanced drawings and proclaimed, "What do you think of this?"

Homer, honest to a fault, said, "I don't know. Vhat's dat?"

"Dis, I mean *this*, is the plan for my new bank. It's grow or die in the banking world these days, and I don't mean to die. See, here is where the present bank stands. Right about here is where you are now sitting. Now, maybe I'd be money ahead just to tear down the whole thing and build a new bank. But there is this little issue of this being an historic building. Now, some of that is nonsense, of course. I mean, the front of the bank is historical, I guess, and is beautiful 1890s-type architecture—I forget what it is called. But (using his fingers as quotation marks) the 'integrity' has already been 'compromised.' Well, I guess I did that when I added that drive-through facility on the side. Anyhow, if the front facade is the important thing, I can get permission to expand in the other direction. I can tear down all the buildings on the other side of this block and expand my bank in that direction. See here? On this page? This is how it'd look. I could more than double my useable space."

"So dis is vhat it would look like, den?"

"You bet. Maybe even nicer—this a preliminary sketch."

Jack, meanwhile, had been examining the plat map. "I didn't realize that you owned all of this block."

Monson gave him a relaxed smile and said, "Well, I don't own all of it just yet, although I have been buying up parcels of property when they come on the market. There are only three lots I don't yet own, but I've made offers on all of them. I'm sure I'll have no trouble acquiring them. This will be the biggest construction in downtown Fergus Falls for more than fifty years."

He dissolved into a self-satisfied chuckle and said, "Now then, Homer and Jack, what can I do for you?"

Homer took two folded sheets of paper from his coat and said, "Dis here's a copy of my vill, and I figgered I wanted to change it."

Monson accepted what was so forcefully thrust upon him but said, "Well, Homer, don't you think this is a matter for your attorney?"

Homer cut him off with a seldom used Norwegian barnyard expression and added "I don't like dem lawyers. Never have. Don't trust 'em. My pa lost most of his farm to dem. No, I know yew don't need one of dem for a vill. How do I know dis? Cus yew said so and yew vitnessed dis first vun. Yew told me to put a copy of it in my safety deposit box and I did dat. Now I vont to change it."

Jack smiled to himself and thought: *This is more like it. Here is where my future could change. Maybe the old man had more property then he let on. He was just babbling about me getting what was coming to me. He wouldn't want to drag me here unless he had more to add, would he?*

Monson shrugged and said, "So, how do you want to change it?"

Homer said, "Yew look right dere on da second page and yew'll see. See dere, right after I had it writ down dat I vas giving everyting to Yack, here. Now, look vat I added. I put in 'except da eighty acres of hay land dat I got from my Pa.' Den I writ, 'I vant to vill dis land to da state of Minnesota for vildlife conservation.'"

Hearing this, Jack felt like he had just gotten kicked in the groin. The old man was giving away his grandfather's land—land that should have come to him. Then, on consideration, he realized what land the old man was talking about and, being in real estate, thought it might be more trouble than it was worth. He was, after all, his uncle's heir, and although he doubted the old fool had ever saved up much money, there were always tales about Norwegian bachelor farmers who were worth a ton of cash. *If he's giving away land, maybe he has a pile of dollars in the bank. It might be cool after all.* With a little windfall, maybe he could invest in a few real estate ventures of his own.

"So den," Homer continued, "If I get bote of yew to sign dis ting, and we put a date on it, vell den, dat's legal, isn't it?"

Monson, recognizing a nice gesture when he saw one, and getting some pleasure out of the fact that Jack would be getting less, replied, "Maybe. I think so. I'm not a lawyer, you know. Tell you what. We can sign it, and date it, and I'll even put a notary stamp on it—I'm still a notary public, you know—and you can stick it in your safety deposit box. I'm going to be kind of busy for the next month or so, but I'll see if I can find out if anything else needs to be done legally. Meanwhile, this would certainly seem to qualify as a legal statement of intent. Is there anything else I can do for you?"

Homer began the lengthy process of standing and said, "No, I suppose dat yust about does it. Tank yew Aldwin."

"My pleasure," he said, and then, rising and summoning the receptionist, added, "Jane, will you take Mr. Grimstead and his nephew down to the safety deposit room?"

Chapter Seven

THE MONTH OF MARCH, IN MINNESOTA, might be an act of survival. If so, April is an act of faith. Some years the faith is rewarded, and the tulips don't have to battle the snow. Other years, blizzards are common, and the snow does not completely disappear from the shaded areas until almost May. The ice on the larger lakes can stay even longer. This year, however, was a grand April. The last of the snow had gone by the end of March and already, in the city of Fergus Falls, people were mowing their lawns.

The sun was brightly shining and the robins were proclaiming that April 14th would be a grand day. Palmer Knutson, however, was not in the mood to enjoy it. It was Good Friday, and although Palmer did not spend the day atoning for past transgressions, the day always made him depressed because he thought, well, maybe he should atone. He recalled a friend of his, a Lutheran pastor he knew in Decorah, Iowa, who always set aside a couple of hours to re-read Elie Wiesel's *Night*. Palmer had read it several times since then, and it had brought home to him the need for all of human-kind to atone.

He tried to cheer himself by thinking about Easter. All the kids would be home. Trygve was already home from St. Olaf College, extending the pleasure of sleeping in his own bed until at least noon. Maj was picking up Amy and the whole family would be together for Easter. Even this depressed him somewhat, since he tended to think about when the kids were all little and there had been that thrill of the Easter Bunny who always visited the Knutson house. Now they would go to church, listen to Rolf do his Easter inspiration, eat a nice ham dinner, and that would be it. It would be nice, of course, but not even one little fight over who bit off the ear of the chocolate rabbit.

Furthermore, ever since that night in March, he had been kicking around the idea of retiring. It was not that he was overworked, and it was not that he disliked his job. It was just that when the idea of retirement came up, he had started to think morbid thoughts along the lines of "three quarters of my life is over. There must be something else I could do while I'm waiting for God."

He parked his Acura in his reserved place in front of the Otter Tail County Justice Center and morosely ambled up to his office. While the Justice Center held the jail and other facilities, the office of the Otter Tail County Sheriff was in the courthouse. It was an impressive building featuring Ionic pillars that gave the building considerable gravitas, especially when it was illuminated at night. Inside, there was marble wainscoating everywhere, and on the floor in the center of the building was embedded a marble eight-pointed star. The Otter theme was found throughout the building, from the door knobs to the interior signs that featured little otters holding up department designations. Over time, Palmer had given his office a personal touch, including a carefully selected leather swivel chair that he considered to be the finest sheriff's chair in the entire world. Behind his chair stood the flag of the United States on the right and the flag of Minnesota on the left, and on the wall hung detailed maps of Minnesota, Otter Tail County, and Norway. On another wall hung a somewhat mangy wolf's pelt backed with dark green felt. He wasn't sure why he liked it—it wasn't as though he had personally shot the poor beast—but it may have had something to do with Ellie's insistence that he get rid of it. Finally, on the wall opposite his desk, was a large oak credenza covered with a beautiful piece of Hardanger lace that had been made by his mother.

He had his *Minneapolis StarTribune* with him and was looking forward to sitting at his desk, drinking coffee, and doing the *New York Times* crossword puzzle —Friday's puzzle was always hard, but it gave him such a feeling of triumph when he completed it. Feelings of triumph at his age were always treasured. Unfortunately for his plans, however, just as he found a pen that actually wrote, Orly Peterson came bounding into the office. Palmer winced. "How does one 'bound' at this time of the day?" he asked himself. He gave him a tired look.

"Hey, Palmer! How yah be? Isn't it a wonderful day? I rode my bike in, and went down along that path by the river. I even saw a goldfinch. You don't see too many of them around these days. So I thought, I'd better tell my bird watching boss about it. You ever ride bike through there?"

Palmer mumbled an unenthusiastic "Used to, I guess—when the kids were smaller. I don't do too much biking these days."

"Well, you ought to. It's good for you." Orly plunked himself down next to Knutson's chair without being asked. Orly Peterson was perhaps the youngest chief deputy in the state of Minnesota. There had been a rash of early retirements among the older deputies over the course of the last two years, and when Palmer had to choose a new chief deputy, he decided to promote from within, and Peterson was the logical choice. Although he sometimes made Palmer feel tired, he had to admire his enthusiasm, his dedication to his physical fitness routine, his regular attendance at the shooting range, his keeping up with the latest computer advances, his networking with other departments, and his growing knowledge of the field of law enforcement. He also knew that Orly loved to wear his uniform pressed and rather tight, to show off his muscles and attract the admiration of women, and that Orly wore his L.A.P.D. sunglasses even during cloudy days because he thought he looked cool. Somehow, the tan uniform, which featured dark brown epaulettes and pocket flaps and a perfectly knotted brown tie, had never looked quite as good on Palmer. Maybe it was his animated brown eyes or his closely cropped brown hair that made the difference, but to Palmer it was merely because he was so disgustingly young. He had been of considerable value to Knutson during a couple of high-profile murder investigations, however, and in the last few years had regarded the young Swede as, well, maybe not quite a friend, but a valued colleague.

Orly noticed that Palmer seemed preoccupied, and said, "Hey, as they said to John Kerry, 'Why the long face?' You need cheering up. I heard a new Norwegian joke yesterday . . ."

Oh, no, how long, oh, Lord, how long? Palmer thought, but instead said, "All right, let me have it."

"So these two Norwegians, Ole and Sven, are up on top of this barn, see, shingling the roof. And so Ole looks over and sees Sven pick up a nail and throw it away, pick up another nail and pound it in, pick up another nail and throw it away, and so on. So Ole, he says, 'Sven, how come you're trowing dose nails avay?' And Sven says, 'Dere no good. Dere heads are on the wrong end.' And Ole he just shakes his head and says, 'Yew know, Sven, I tink yer da dumbest man I ever met. You don't trow dem avay, dere for da other side of da barn.'"

Peterson's snickering temporarily obscured the fact that Knutson was not laughing. "What's the matter? You heard it before?"

"Matter of fact, I have. And I remember just where, too. It was over forty years ago, in confirmation class. It was the only joke that old Pastor Ringdahl ever told in his life. The only difference is that then it was about two Swedes."

"All right, now I know something's the matter. Everything all right at home? Ellie okay? Anything wrong with the kids?"

"No, no, everything's fine. I just don't like this time of the year. I know spring has sprung and all that, but have you seen all the posters—gas stations, the post office, the bank, the supermarket, everywhere—that are advertizing farm auctions? I mean, we were able to hang onto our farm when I was a kid, but just barely. And now, well, you look around, and there are hardly any small farmers left. Go for a drive in the country and there are people living in only one out of four farmsteads. The school bus used to go five miles out of town and return with a load of kids. Now they have a route four times as long. Rural areas are becoming depopulated, and every time I see a poster for a farm auction I think either some old guy hung on until he died, and there will never be a farm there again, or that some young guy finally came to grips with his failure.

"Now, other than nostalgia for the old days, do you know why I hate that? It's because we often have to be the agent of this change. I've got four deputies right now that do little else except serve papers. That's bad enough, but what's worse is when we have to go evict someone, take over their property for debts, and hold a sheriff's sale.

"So I've been thinking, do I really want to do this anymore? Back in the sixties, we really did have this notion of a calling, of helping people. I thought I was able to help by being a compassionate law enforcement officer—and let me tell you, at that time that was sort of an oxymoron—like 'army intelligence' or, as Ellie would say, 'Compassionate Conservatism.' But what am I doing now? I'm a pencil pusher and a paper shuffler. I spend far more time with budgets than anything else. I have to show up at nauseating events like that Congressman Paulson's dog-and-pony show last month. I have become a member of permanent committees. Committees! If you had asked me about committees thirty-five years ago, I would have sneered with contempt. Now I chair them. I used to feel I was doing something useful when I would make out roster assignments, but now I've got you doing that. I don't mean to sound sour, I mean, I'm my own boss—the only time I ever really have to show up is to be sworn in—and the pay is, I must admit, pretty good."

This was a side of the sheriff that Orly rarely saw, and listening to him, he felt closer to his boss. "So, is there anything else you would like to do."

Knutson took off his glasses and rubbed the bridge of his nose. "Well, that's the thing, isn't it? I don't know. What the department accomplishes in the course of the year is necessary and we do it well. But personally . . . You know, Ellie thinks I secretly want to be like John Rebus."

Orly scowled, trying to place the name and assuming it was either an early quarterback for the Vikings or one of the sheriff's predacessors. "Who?"

"He's this inspector in the Edinburgh police, the main character in the novels of Ian Rankin. Now there's a tough cop! But I think Ellie's wrong."

"How so?"

"I really want to be like Diamond—he's the inspector who is the creation of the novelist Peter Lovesley."

"Why do you want to be like him?," asked Peterson, now somewhat intrigued by the workings of an elderly mind.

"Because if I were John Rebus, I would have to live in cold rainy Scotland, whereas if I were Diamond, I could do my detecting in beautiful Bath, England, which, from my travel literature and the Lovesley books, sounds like one of the most beautiful towns in the world."

Peterson chuckled and said, "That sounds like a good enough reason to me. I wouldn't mind being a cop for Hawaii 5-0. But you'd still be in the law enforcement business."

"Yah, I know. And that still means, um—not to get too maudlin, philosophical, or sentimental—trying to make this world a better place. And I don't know if that's possible. I just feel, I don't know, so pessimistic today. Do you know what Winston Churchill called his bouts of depression? 'The Black Dog.' The 'black dog' seems to be biting today. I was watching CNN this morning, trying to get enough energy to get out of bed. The Sunnis hate the Shi'ites, the Shi'ites hate the Sunnis, they both hate the Kurds, but then, so do the Turks. India hates Pakistan and vice-versa. They all hate the Jews, and everyone in the world, it seems, hates Americans. And you think, 'Hey man, I've never done anything to you.' But then they say, 'Yes you did. You paid taxes that bought the airplane that dropped the bomb on my village and killed my entire family.' And he's right, in a way, and that gets us back to the Vietnam era thinking and it's like we haven't learned a damn thing."

Orly Peterson, who once would have snickered behind the sheriff's back while listening to this type of introspection, had grown to admire the depths of Knutson's moral wrestling matches with himself. Now he said, "Yeah, I guess you're right. But aren't you the one who always says justice must begin at home, think globally but act locally, and all that stuff? As long as you are doing what you can, you know, I mean, all that Camus existentialism stuff, you know?"

"Yah," Knutson relented, "but that's part of the problem, too. I don't know if you heard, but old Homer Grimstead died. Did you know him? Anyway, I saw him a week ago, and I thought, 'He doesn't look quite the ticket,' and so I asked him how he was doing and he mumbled something about having felt better and so I asked him if he had gone to the doctor and he just said, 'Doctors don't know nothing' and shuffled off. So he died on Wednesday. His doctor said he had 'cancer of the everything.' Here today, gone tomorrow.

"So, anyway, he's barely cold when Carolyn Dahl starts telling everyone that Homer had left eighty acres of land to be used by her group, the local Otter Tail County Bird Watchers and Conservation Society. And just when everyone thought that was nice, albeit a little strange, Chief Foss starts telling everyone that Homer had left that property to the Fergus Falls Fin and Feather Club. Who knows what the truth is? But, unfortunately, Carolyn Dahl ran into the chief in, of all places, the produce section at Sunmart. From what I heard, they almost started throwing vegetables at each other. Meanwhile, Ellie went to Nora's Knitting Nook yesterday and talked to Jack Grimstead—he's Homer's nephew and apparently he bought the business. No one can figure out why—So Ellie imparted condolences to Jack Grimstead on the death of his uncle and, since she is a bird watcher, and Jack was a bird watcher, said it was so nice that Homer had given that land to them to preserve the prairie chickens. Jack Grimstead said he knew nothing about that. He allowed as to how maybe his uncle had talked about giving it to the state, but didn't know for certain if that had been finalized and that as far as he knew that land might be coming to him. So now we got the bird protectors mad at the bird shooters and they are both mad at Jack Grimstead, who claims to know nothing about it.

"Ellie told Carolyn Dahl what Jack had said, and she immediately set out to prove her point and said that she knew that Aldwin Monson knew all about it and so she marched over to the bank and demanded a meeting with Monson. Well, you probably heard what happened to him. It turns out she picked a real bad time to confront him, because just as she demanded to speak to him, the doors to the bank opened and the emergency paramedics burst in. Monson had collapsed on his way down to the vault, someone had called 911, and nobody knew what was happening. Carolyn, oblivious to what was going on, became incensed at being ignored. They carried Monson out on a gurney right in front of her, but because he had an oxygen mask on, she didn't know who it was. The whole thing apparently was distasteful in the extreme.

"Then there's the whole business of where the ethanol plant is going to be built. Monson apparently thought he had the perfect site and was ready to set up a deal. He was getting pressure from realtors and lawyers and stockholders. He had also let it slip that he was planning a big addition to his bank, and a couple of property holders on that block behind the bank were claiming that he was strong-arming them to sell. I mean, the guy was under a lot of pressure.

"Anyhow, they get Monson to the hospital, and he regains consciousness for a bit and manages to gasp out 'Tell Jack . . .' And that's it. He had joined the choir invisible. His secretary, who had ridden along in the ambulance, wailed, 'They killed Aldwin!'"

"Wow," said the transfixed but bewildered chief deputy, "do you think there's any truth to that? I mean, him dying a day after old Grimstead, knowing Grimstead's intentions, and all that? Are we talking murder? Double murder?"

"Funny you should say that. It's the first thing I thought of. And, of course, that can't be. Grimstead, apparently, had been living on borrowed time for weeks. Monson had a bad ticker and had been under considerable stress. It has to be just a coincidence. But that's part of the reason why I feel depressed this morning. Here are two natural deaths of two elderly gentlemen. What do I think? Murder! What's the world coming to? What am I becoming? I'm sure the secretary merely meant that all those who were putting pressure on Monson were somehow responsible. Nah, it's just life, er, in this case, death."

After a long pause, Knutson said, "Nevertheless, it's just more of that unsettled feeling that I have. Remember that line, 'By the pricking of my thumbs, something evil this way comes?' Well, I feel like that. Know where that's from, by the way?"

Orly smirked and said, "As a matter of fact, I do. It's Shakespeare."

"Very good, Orly. It's from the *Merchant of Venice* and also part of the title of an Agatha Christie book."

Supercillious expressions should be reserved for the elderly. On youth, they look merely smug. "Actually, it isn't."

"It is too. I just read that book when I took my vacation last summer."

"No, I'll accept your word for it that there's a book of that title by Agatha Christie, but the quotation is from

Macbeth, and it isn't 'something evil this way comes,' it is 'something wicked this way comes.'"

"You sure?"

"Yup."

"How do you know?" asked the sheriff, who had an inflated opinion as to the superiority of his own education compared to those of more recent graduates.

"Matter of fact, I've been in *Macbeth*?"

"You? When was that?"

"When I was going to Fergus Falls State. I played the role of Duncan. I was pretty good, too, if I say so myself."

"Amazing. 'Is this a dagger I see before me?' Wait a minute, that was *MacBeth* himself who said that, wasn't it? Did Rolf Norson direct that?"

"As a matter of fact, he did. And he said I did a good job."

"I wonder how come I didn't see that?" Knutson said, his 'black dog' seemingly vanquished. "I try to never miss one of Norson's plays. He is a real treasure for that university. I remember once when he did *Merry Wives of Windsor*. Now, that's not one of Shakespeare's best. Nobody does it anymore. I think he staged it just to show everyone what he could do with it. It was a triumph. It got entered into some kind of national competition and I seem to remember it did very well. Huh, you were Duncan. I was in *Julius Caesar* in high school. Were you in any other plays at F.F.S.U?"

The talk of college ways and college days and college plays did succeed in diverting Palmer's thoughts.

Nevertheless, he could not completely ignore the "pricking of his thumbs" and the unfortunate coincidence of two apparently unrelated deaths.

Chapter Eight

T HREE THOUSAND YEARS AGO, the supposedly blind poet Homer enthralled his listeners when he began another episode of the adventures of Odysseus with the words, "And when the early-born, rosy-fingered dawn appeared." Palmer Knutson remembered these words from *The Odyssey* as he gazed at the dawn of April 15.

The whole plan for carpooling to Kettle Drummer Prairie had not been organized as successfully as Ellie had hoped. Four cars had been employed to transport ten people to the blind in anticipation of clandestinely viewing the mating habits of the prairie chicken. Palmer explained that, as sheriff, it was necessary that he have access to a vehicle in case of an emergency, and Ellie accepted that logic. But Palmer's Acura TL followed Carolyn Dahl's Lexus SUV, and there were only two people in a vehicle that could have transported a little league team. Behind Palmer and Ellie came the white Dodge belonging to Ione Schultz who was accompanied, as usual, by her two friends, Beverly Peterson and Cheryl Nyhus. Bringing up the rear was the Ford pickup of Earl Moen.

The planning for the outing had been complete until yesterday when Roxanne Dahl, Carolyn's middle child, had decided, without being invited by her mother, that she would accompany the Otter Tail County Bird Watching and Conservation Society on their grand outing. It was a decision that was popular with no one.

In the white Dodge, Beverly Peterson complained, "Can you believe it? She has never come to a single meeting, doesn't know a bird from an airplane, and she just horns in on our best outing ever. Why couldn't her mother make her stay home?"

"Hah!" Ione Schultz said, "Her mother hasn't known what to do with her for twenty years. I kind of feel sorry for Carolyn. I mean, her oldest child, Marshall, went straight into med school and is now a successful doctor, her youngest kid, Julieann, just graduated from Concordia College with honors—you can't say she can't raise decent children."

"She sure failed when it came to Roxanne," interjected Cheryl Nyhus. "I do believe that she is perhaps the most obnoxious person I have ever met."

They continued in this mutually agreed upon character assassination all the way to the nature preserve. The three women had been childhood friends, united in a shared appreciation for each other's intelligence and sense of humor. All three had grown up to be beautiful and successful women and had gone their separate ways in life. But widowhood, divorce, and retirement had brought them all back to Fergus Falls, and they soon renewed that deep friendship that had existed fifty years earlier. They certainly were of one mind when it came to Roxanne Dahl. "So how long," Beverly asked as they neared their objective, "can you refrain from slapping her? I give myself twenty minutes."

Cheryl cautioned, "Now, now. That just wouldn't do. You know, Carolyn does have a cross to bear with her daughter. Tolerance, ladies. Tolerance. Relax. And I brought a full quart thermos of coffee to help us relax."

Ione asked, "Is there any brandy in it?"

"Well, yes, now that you mention it," Cheryl admitted, "I did perk it up a bit with some brandy."

"Is there any coffee in it?"

"Well, a little.

"Could be a fun morning after all," Beverly admitted.

In the pickup, Earl Moen was bellyaching. "You're going to owe me for this, Selma. I don't mind getting up a little early, but this is practically the middle of night. Now I can see it if it were the opening of the fishing season or something important. But watching a bunch of birds hop around? Don't they have something like this on the Nature Channel? And I'm almost the only man in this dumb parade."

Selma replied, "I would certainly consider Sheriff Knutson a man, wouldn't you"

"Yah, I 'spose. And that's the only thing that got me to agree to this silliness. I figger if he can take it, I can too. But who is that awful girl with Carolyn Dahl?"

"That's her daughter, so be nice to her. Carolyn is always nice to us."

"Uffda, that's going to be hard to do," Earl mumbled.

In the Acura, Palmer and Ellie Knutson were getting to know Stover Stordahl. Palmer had picked him up in front of his apartment. Stover had, as usual, been puffing on a Tareyton as he waited for his ride. Before allowing him in, Palmer sternly warned Stover that he did not allow smoking in his car. Stover had replied, "Of course not not, Sheriff. I never smoke in cars."

And that had been it. Palmer and Ellie soon grew accustomed to Stover's unusual speech pattern, and were pleasantly surprised to find out just how much Stover knew about birds. He talked at length about his bird books, and as he did so, confident of his subject matter, his stutter was barely noticeable. The only time he reverted to his excitable state was when he asked Ellie about the young woman driving Carolyn Dahl's car.

"Ah, that would be her older daughter. She has been staying with her mother for the last few weeks while she, as Carolyn put it, 'sorts things out.'"

"Nasty girl girl," said Stover, adding a few short staccato obscenities.

In Carolyn Dahl's Lexus, Roxanne Dahl was accusing her mother of 'eco-fascism.' "I mean, nature is wonderful and all that. I wouldn't be along if I didn't basically agree with all that you are doing. But do we have to do it so early? Those birds have a whole mating season, and you can't tell me that they only do it at sunrise."

She truly was an 'unlovely' woman. Carolyn was beautiful. Roxanne's sister was beautiful and her brother was handsome. It seemed that every negative trait that the Dahl family had—going back centuries in Norway—was magnified in Roxanne. It is often said that beauty is only skin deep, and if so, shouldn't that also apply to ugliness? In Roxanne's case, it was not so.

Truth be told, if one didn't know Roxanne, she might not have appeared ugly. She did have a certain understanding of basic hygiene, and her hair was quite nice. Her face was nicely proportioned, and her brown eyes looked like those of Bambi. The effect was ruined, however, when she attempted to smile. Her two front teeth were divided by a gap that increased from top to bottom. It was a problem that any orthodontist could have repaired with braces, and the Dahl family could easily have afforded them, but Roxanne had thought braces to be ugly, refused to go through "the ordeal," and justified her cowardice by claiming that the look gave her a beautiful identity. Well, it gave her an identity, at least. As a result, she did not smile very much, and her mouth seemed tiny and her thin lips seemed permanently pursed. An unkind classmate had once said, "her mouth is so little she has to eat peas one at a time."

She did, however, attract the attention of at least two people. One was her college advisor. He was a psychology professor who believed that her aggressive rudeness was really the result of deep seated feelings of inferiority. For three years he thought he was making progress with her until he finally decided, along with everyone else, that her aggressive rudeness was "just the result of a rotten personality." The other person in her life was Duane Marks. Marks was an introverted student who longed for the ability to speak out. In class discussions, while other students were revolted by Roxanne's hostile attacks, he defended her. She recognized that he was interested in her, and since no one else had ever evinced such attraction, she played him like an energetic salmon in the Columbia river. She was convinced it was a sexual attraction, although this would seem unlikely to anyone who objectively evalu-ated her appeal. She was convinced, however, that being flat chested was the new mark of femininity and openly ridiculed women who were more endowed. She toler-ated Marks, and that was enough for him. When Roxanne went off to "get a Ph.D." in psychology, Marks meekly followed her to Vanderbilt University, then the University of Tennessee, then the University of Northern Iowa. The credits had added up, but there was no degree in sight. Finally, she decided that the real thing that was holding her back was Duane Marks. She dropped him like a wet bar of soap, dropped out of her classes, and went back to mother to reevaluate her career. It was a decision that Carolyn regretted.

By the time they reached Kettle Drummer Prairie it was light enough to turn off the headlights. The four vehicles parked, and everyone attempted to exit their vehicles as quietly as possible. Everyone, that is, except Roxanne Dahl, who slammed her door with a violence that made everyone wince. Amid admonitions for silence, the bird watchers advanced in search of their prey.

It must be said that it was all they ever hoped it would be. The males lifted their tails, lowered their wings, stuck out their necks, and raised their pinnae feathers above their heads. They puffed our their orange air sacs and began to stamp their feet and to boom. It was a sound somewhat like that made by blowing air across the top of an open bottle, but it was much louder, and it has been claimed one could hear that sound two miles away. The females remained on the fringes, seemingly with eyes only for the males. Adopting their most menacing poses, the males began to face off against each other, defending their spot on the lek. As a female appeared interested, the action seemed to intensify. In sight and sound it was a magnificent display.

In the blind, all was quiet. Everyone held their breath. Digital cameras were aimed and clicked and camcorders captured the sight and sounds of marvelous nature. Cheryl uncapped the coffee and poured. Ione audibly gasped and Beverly winced and smiled at Cheryl. Unfortunately, this bucolic commune with nature was interrupted by Roxanne Dahl.

Beginning in a loud and admiring whisper, she said: "Oooh-aah, look at that boy chicken over there. He's strutting around like he's got something to show.

He thinks he's hot stuff. And look over there on the edge of the clearing. That girl chicken is giving him the eye. Watch it, honey, you know what he's got in mind." Her voice got louder as she said, "And listen to that big boomer. How can that sweetie-pie resist that, huh? Nothing like a little x-rated nature show, huh? And look over there. There's a couple of big boy chickens who look like they're going to have a fight. Don't you just love it, girls, when boys fight over you?"

Palmer reflected that Roxanne was extremely unlikely ever to have had that particular experience, but held his tongue. The others in the blind attempted to politely shush her into silence. It did not produce the desired results.

"Oh, don't be such prudes," she retorted. "You know exactly what they're up to, and we're like a bunch of teenage boys trying to peek into the girl's locker room. The difference is, these guys seem pretty sure that they're going to get lucky."

She kept on in her annoying fashion, rather enjoying the effect she was having on everyone. Stover Stordahl was not in the least affected by Roxanne's blithering nonsense, for he was much too absorbed in the scene about which he had read with such interest. Unfortunately, it was at times of such excitement that Tourette's syndrome can unexpectly manifest itself. As Roxanne finished one of her inane observations, Stover blurted out the f-word three times in a rapid staccato.

For reasons best known to herself, Roxanne interpreted this to be an overly aggressive and crude suggestion from a man to a woman. She screamed, "Oh, gross!"

In one second, the booming of the prairie chickens stopped completely.

Perhaps, for all of mankind, there are those moments in the life of individuals when the timing of events, haphazard or as a result of a misalignment of the cosmos, conspire against them. Earl Moen had not had his usual breakfast. He had, in the short minutes before departure, gulped down two pop tarts and washed them down with coffee. His intestines had been growling for some time. *Surely*, he thought, *in the breezy blind no one would notice if he were to relieve the pressure.* He thought it an appropriate time to break wind, and believed he could do it with sneaky silence. Perhaps at an another time, in another dimension, his subterfuge would have been successful. It was not. In the silence of the prairie following Roxanne's outburst, there arose a noise that shook the walls of the blind and sounded to the ears of the prairie chickens to be the roll of distant thunder.

Roxanne shreaked again. "Oh gross! That's the last straw!" She stormed out of the blind as the prairie chickens scattered. She ran to her mother's Lexus, started it up, and began to tear down the trail. In a last bit of unfortunate timing, a startled prairie chicken flew into her path. The entire party heard a loud thump and saw feathers fly as the Lexus sped away. The members of the Otter Tail County Bird Watching and Conservation Society dourly made their way to the scene of the accident and looked down at the late bird. Nobody had much to say about it, until finally Earl remarked, "Anybody feel like chicken stew tonight. It would be a shame to waste it."

CHAPTER NINE

CHUCK AND SANDY FARNHORST were on their way to Glacier National Park. It was the shakedown cruise for the brand new Winnebago. It was Chuck's pride and joy, the pay-off for all those years working on the assembly line of Harley-Davidson Motorcycles. His former workers back in Milwaukee were in awe of its majesty, and appreciated the Green Bay Packers decals tastefully affixed to every side. They had made good time on the first day, and had camped out at the rest stop just east of Alexandria, Minnesota. They had decided to put on a few miles before they stopped for breakfast from their well-stocked mini-refrigerator.

Just because Chuck wanted to "chuck-it," (as he interminably proclaimed) and retire, Sandy saw no reason why she should give up her profitable real estate business. As a sop to her, and to ease his conscience about buying an outrageously expensive motor home, Chuck had promised her a portable office. From the rest stop, they had pulled into the parking lot of the Holiday Inn of Alexandria, where Sandy could access the wireless system of the motel and check her e-mail. At six o'clock in the morning on Easter Sunday, however, she did not expect a great volume of business. This proved to be the case, but as long as she had a good signal, she decided to make the best use of it. Sandy had taken to technology with far greater ardor and skill than Chuck, and began to call up information on her lap top on every town on Interstate 94, downloaded the information into her computer, and in the process created a modern gazetteer. When she told Chuck about the attractions of Alexandria, therefore, it had been necessary to drive into the city to see the statue of the big Viking on the shores of Lake La Homme Dieu. They marveled at it. It was indeed worth the stop. It was a shame that the museum was not open yet, because Chuck would have liked to have seen the Kensington Rune Stone. But it was hours away from opening time, and Chuck hoped to be well into North Dakota by then.

"Just think," Sandy said as they got back on the interstate and she turned her attention once again to the information stored on her laptop, "It says here that a bunch of Vikings from—where did they come from, anyway, Norway?—anyway, they came here in 1362 and carved on this rock just to tell the world that they had been here. Really makes you think, doesn't it?"

"Yup," Chuck sagely acknowledged, "this is really Viking territory—sword in one hand, football in the other."

"You know, that reminds me," Sandy interjected, "I was gonna ask you. Last night, when we were at that rest stop, were you worried that anyone would do anything to our motor home, what with all those Packers stickers all over it?"

"Huh? No, of course not. People don't vandalize something just because they don't like a football team. Don't be silly."

"Well, I happen to remember that time you snapped a radio antenna off a car just because it had a Chicago Bears sticker on the bumper."

"Yeah, well, I mean, that was the Bears, and the car was parked right down town where we were having that Super Bowl victory party, and, you know . . ." After an uncomfortable pause, Chuck quietly admitted, "Still, I guess I shouldn'ta done it. I'm a little bit ashamed about that, to tell you the truth. But these are Minnesotans. I mean, they're not Bear fans. We don't have to worry about them." Chuck had spoken with confidence, but did not tell Sandy that the first thing he had done that morning was to carefully check the motor home for damage.

"Besides, nobody's gonna attack a Winnebago. You know, that salesman where we got this thing was telling me that in the early days of the company, anybody who lived in Forest City, Iowa—that's where they are made—could just decide to go on a trip and call the company and get a unit to deliver. If you wanted to go to Boston, you just called them and asked if they had a motor home that they needed to deliver to Massachusetts. They would pay for the gas and give you enough money to get home again. They got their Winnebago delivered, you got a free trip! Heck of a deal! Too bad they didn't let us deliver Harleys that way."

They rolled in comfort past the exits for Barrett and Evansville and Dalton, and started seeing signs advertising what Fergus Falls had to offer. "What can you tell me about Fergus Falls, then, dear? Any more Viking statues?

"Maybe I should look up to see if they have any Catholic churches. It is Easter, you know, and we really should go to mass."

Chuck, with a tone of voice that implied, with reason, that this was an issue that had already been abundantly debated, mumbled, "Yeah, well, we went last year, and we'll go next year. Nobody's gonna tell the priest in Milwaukee that we weren't there this morning."

Sandy primly replied, "That's not the point." But she dropped the issue and soon her fingers flew across the keyboard and she announced, "Well, they do have a statue of a big otter. Fergus Falls is the county seat of Otter Tail County, it seems. It's a town of almost fourteen thousand people, and is the home of Fergus Falls State University."

"Oh, yeah," Chuck interrupted, "The Fergus Falls Flying Falcons, good football team. I've read about them. What else is there?"

"They included some pictures on their website. Looks like a nice town. Says they have a five-block river walk, and there are five lakes within the city. And it talks about their cultural center and things like that."

"This here big otter, is that near the highway? I'd like to see that."

"Says it's in Adams Park, and that's, let's see . . . no, it's not real handy. We don't have to see all these monuments, do we?"

As they approached the Fergus Falls exits, Chuck observed, "Well, they got a Target Store and a Wal-Mart. You don't need much more than that. What's that big building on the north edge of town?"

"Let's see here," mumbled Sandy. "I think that would be the Regional Treatment Center. That sometimes means it is a mental institution."

"Look at the size of that thing! If you weren't loony when you went in, I'll bet you would be by the time you came out! We should stop for breakfast pretty soon. What's the next town? Anything to see there?"

Sandy checked the map. "Um . . . I guess it would be Rothsay. Let me see if I can find out anything about it." After an amazingly short time, she said, "Ah, here it is. Rothsay—town of about five hundred. Says here it is the Prairie Chicken Capital of Minnesota."

"So, what the hell is a prairie chicken ?"

"It seems to be an orange and white and brown bird—there's a picture of it here. Wait a minute, this is a picture of a statue! There's a guy standing under it. The 'world's largest prairie chicken'—well, I would guess so. It looks huge! It's fourteen feet tall and weighs 9,200 pounds—officially dedicated in 1976. I wonder if it was some kind of Bicentennial event?"

"We gotta see that! Is it near an exit? Might be a good place to stop for breakfast."

Chuck strained his eyes for the next several miles as the interstate took them out of the semi-wooded lake region to the broad prairie. "Well, here comes the exit, I don't see any big chicken. Wait a minute! Look, just beyond that gas station. That must be it!"

Chuck drove the Winnebago off the interstate and crossed to the other side, easily pulling into the small but deserted parking lot. He shut off the engine and eagerly hopped out, saying, "Grab the camera. You ain't gonna see this every day."

Sandy was less enthusiastic. "Why do I have to get out and look at it. I can see it just fine from here. We're not exactly talking about Michaelangelo's David, here, you know. It is basically a big pile of cement."

"Are you going to be like this for the whole trip? All right, stay there. Gimme the camera. I want to get a close-up look-see." He angrily stomped off in the direction of the big bird, regretting within three steps that he hadn't put on his jacket. A second later, he forgot the cold, as he saw what was undoubtedly a human being lying just under the giant beak. He rushed forward and saw the dried blood that had oozed out of the head of the unfortunate ex-human. Chuck's jaw dropped and for five seconds he gazed in horror. Other than funerals, it was the first corpse he had ever seen. In a panic, he ran back to the Winnebago.

"Gimme the cell phone," he yelled, "I gotta call 911. It looks like someone's been pecked to death."

CHAPTER TEN

THE APRIL SUN STREAMED INTO the all-season porch as Palmer Knutson, with a satisfied grunt, sat down with a cup of coffee and the Sunday *Minneapolis StarTribune*. Life didn't get any better than that! The coffee was magnificent, as Palmer knew it would be, ever since he had perfected the right amount of coffee beans to add to his Cuisinart coffeemaker. It had been Palmer and Ellie's surprise gift to each other. They bought it together and expressed surprise together when they had opened the box last Christmas Eve. It was marvelous. One just added water and the beans and pushed the button and everything whirred and dripped and soon the heavenly aroma of fresh coffee filled the whole house.

Palmer loved Sunday mornings. He still had on his Minnesota Vikings pajamas under his rather ratty velour robe. On his feet were two giant pink bunny slippers. His elder daughter, Maj, had given them to her father on Christmas Eve as a joke, and as a little reminder of when she was a little girl and had loved her bunny slippers. Palmer had swallowed hard and put on a false smile and thanked her. Then, to show he was a good sport, he put them on. Everyone laughed and, as the evening went on, he rather forgot that he was wearing them. When he took them off to go to bed, he was amazed to find how toasty his feet felt. Now they were an everyday necessity, and he thought they were cool. Imagine what the villains of Otter Tail County would say if they saw their sheriff in bunny slippers! Besides, it was Easter. What could be more appropriate. He was hoping to see Maj's face when she noticed he was wearing them.

Ellie was still upstairs. While laying in bed, Palmer had checked the weather channel and then surfed to see what else was on cable. He didn't get by the Audrey Hepburn movie fast enough, however, and now Ellie was engrossed. There was still some time before he had to dress for church. However comfy he felt, missing church was not an option. It was what one did on Easter Sunday when one's brother, the Reverend Rolf Knutson, was the pastor of the largest Lutheran Church in Fergus Falls. Perhaps Rolf wouldn't notice that he wasn't there, but Palmer always felt that he did, and, in fact, Rolf usually did notice. Palmer had always been rather in awe of his brother. He seemed so sure of everything, and preached the Gospel as, well, the "Gospel truth." Palmer considered himself to be a Christian, of course, and a Lutheran one at that, but he had to admit he didn't really believe everything his brother proclaimed from the pulpit. He wished that he could have a man-to-man talk with Rolf to ask him what he really did believe, but his brother was ten years older, and, well, they had never had that kind of relationship. In fact, Palmer may have been surprised in the course of such a conversation that would never take place. Reverend Knutson was highly educated, obsessed with reading theology, and realized that there were some things that need not be said. There were things in theology that were disturbing, and no one in his parish ever really wanted to be disturbed. He was eloquent, he was socially conscious, and with his magnificent bearing he had been called the Lutheran Pope of western Minnesota. Palmer was proud of him, but regretted that he had never actually sat down to have a beer with him.

He skipped over the depressing news of the end of the season for the Minnesota Timberwolves and the upcoming Vikings' draft. There were more important things. The baseball season was almost two weeks old, and already it was apparent that the Twins were going to need more than great fielding and decent pitching. They needed a bat—a power hitter—somebody who would scare opposing pitchers. Palmer thought, "they shoulda traded for . . ."

His rumination was interrupted by the telephone. His first thought was that it had to be for one of the kids. Who would call him at a time like this? Then, with dread, he remembered what his job was. It could be official. He answered with an uncommittal "Hello?"

The voice on the other end was brassy and impatient. "Palmer, we got a problem."

Palmer responded with, "Is this Orly?"

"Yah, look, um, I just got a call from Curtis, who is on duty this morning. He wasn't sure what to do and didn't know whether to bother you or not. There's been a murder."

"A murder! Why wouldn't he call me right away?"

"It seems there's some question of jurisdiction. A body was found under that big prairie chicken in Rothsay. Technically, that's in Wilkin County. Across the road there's that big truck stop—that's in Otter Tail County. The guy who discovered the body called 911 and reported he was in Rothsay and so the call went first down to Breckenridge. They called down there, and all they got was an answering machine. I don't know what's going on. They're usually pretty much on top of things, but it's a small county and it was six o'clock on Easter Sunday morning. Anyhow, when they didn't get anybody, they called us. Curtis figured he'd better get to the scene, a rare bit of clear thinking on his part, so he left immediately and secured the area. He's out there now, wondering what to do next."

"Is he alone?" Palmer asked, with a certain amount of dread.

"Far as I know. The people who discovered the body were traveling in one of those big Winnebago things and he told them to get back in their mobile home and wait. He said a couple of people from the truck stop had seen his car with the lights blinking and stopped over for a gawk. But he should be able to handle that."

"Any idea who it is?"

"Well, Curtis had to make sure he was dead, and in so doing, he said he thinks he has seen him around town, but he said the poor sap's head was bashed in and there was blood on his face, so he couldn't really identify him. If he is from Fergus Falls, we probably better handle the case, even though it might technically be a hundred yards away from Otter Tail County.

"Yah, I suppose. Geez, remember that case with that big concrete loon near Vergus? Now we have to deal with a big prairie chicken. I suppose I'd better get over there. I should shower and shave and get dressed. It doesn't sound like the victim will be in a hurry to go anywhere. Why don't you get over there and find out what happened, and I'll get there as soon as I can. See yah."

Palmer hung up the phone, looked longingly at his newspaper, and regretted that he hadn't even had a chance to start the crossword puzzle. He laboriously climbed the stairs, feeling older than he had just minutes before, and informed Ellie that he had been called out on a case. It was an occasion for wearing a uniform, and as Palmer carefully did up his shirt buttons, Ellie knew there was something unpleasant about the occasion.

"What kind of case," she asked, with one eye on Audrey Hepburn.

"Murder. I don't know who. I don't know how. I certainly don't know why, but I do know where. He seems to have been killed under that big prairie chicken in Rothsay—No, don't say it—it is just a coincidence. It is not revenge for what Roxanne Dahl did yesterday. Anyway, I don't know when I'll be back. You'll have to to go church without me, and good luck in getting Trygve out of bed. Oh, and give my regards to Rolf."

"But what about breakfast?"

Palmer sighed. Easter breakfast had always been a family tradition. Hot cross buns, bacon, scrambled eggs—the one time he could inhale the colesterol and not feel guilty. With extreme pain and self-pity he said: "I guess you'd better just go ahead without me."

PALMER EASED HIS ACURA OUT of the garage and into the street. "What should it be today?" he thought. He rejected his Who—Live at Leeds and his old reliable Jethro Tull music because, well, it was Easter Sunday. Instead, he selected his Mozart CD, which was always disc six in his dashboard changer. Soon the world's greatest music from the world's greatest composer filled the car. Of all the duties as sheriff, this was the one he hated the most. Violent death. Had he somehow failed? He remembered the uneasiness he had felt just two days earlier.

Arriving at the murder scene, he pulled into the parking lot next to the huge mobile home. Two anxious faces watched him as he made his way to the crime scene where Curtis stood uselessly and Orly was taking pictures of the body. He called to Orly, "You know who it is?"

"No, but I think I've seen him before. Judging from the wound and the blood near the head, I don't think he was attacked here. There was some blood on the ground, which indicates he continued to bleed and was alive at the time when he was dumped here."

Palmer got closer and his heart sank. "Oh, no. Not him. Why would anyone want to kill him?" A sadness such as he had hardly ever known took over. He turned his head and walked back. A sickening pain seemed to convulse his entire body.

Orly sensed this this was no ordinary reaction. He walked over to Palmer and gently said, "Who is it?"

The bright morning sun burned through his tears as he gasped, "One of the most innocent men I have ever known. That is, or was, Stover Stordahl."

Chapter Eleven

S O WHAT TO WE DO NEXT?" Orly asked. "Somebody will have to notify the next of kin. Any idea who that would be?"

They were sitting in Knutson's office, with Palmer leaning his head into both hands. They had stayed at the site of the discovery of the body for several hours. A scene of the crime crew had arrived to comb the area for any evidence and had found none. There may once have been useable tire tracks in the gravel of the parking lot near the prairie chicken, but the huge Winnebago had obliterated whatever might have been there. An ambulance had arrived to take the body of the unfortunate Stover Stordahl back to Fergus Falls. After taking their statements, and getting an approximate itinerary of their future travels, the sheriff allowed Chuck and Sandy Fahnhorst to continue on their way. While waiting for the scene of the crime team to finish their work, Orly and Palmer had gone across the road to the truck stop for a less than memorable lunch. The food may have been acceptable, but Palmer couldn't taste it. In truth, he would not have enjoyed Ellie's fine ham dinner, either. Finally, they had driven back in their respective vehicles and gloomily made their way back to Palmer's office.

"Yah, I asked him about that just yesterday. The only relative he has left is his mother. She lives in some kind of retirement home on Battle Lake. I suppose I'll have to drive over there and tell her. Unless you are volunteering to do it."

"No thanks. That's a job nobody wants. Besides, you are much better at it than I would be."

"I don't know about that, but, unfortunately, I'm more experienced at it than you are. But still, there are no good words to say to a mother whose son has been brutally murdered."

"Yeah, well, without meaning to appear insensitive, better you than me. Got any idea yet on how you want to pursue the investigation?"

"Well," Palmer began as he leaned back on his chair, "on the face of it, you ask yourself who would ever want to murder a harmless soul like Stover? The answer, of course, would appear to be 'nobody.' Clearly, the most important issue of this case will be motive. Unless this killing was the work of a deranged lunatic— which frankly would be the only thing that would make sense—somebody doing a 'thrill killing' or, worse yet, some serial killer doing his thing. But we have determined that, although he may have died under the prairie chicken, he was not attacked there. A random killer doesn't take great pains to move the body. I suppose the first thing we have to do is to find out who would benefit from killing Stover. We can probably rule out mundane things like a 'love triangle,' and he certainly didn't seem to have an estate worth inheriting. So why? It would seem to me that the most obvious reason was to keep him from doing something or keep him from telling something. Did someone have to shut his mouth? To keep him from telling what?"

Orly nodded seriously. "Do you think there is any significance in where the body was discovered? It was clearly put there to be found. Just two days ago, you were worrying about the growing discontent over land set aside for prairie chickens, and he was part of that. Now we find him under the biggest prairie chicken of them all."

"You know, odd as that may sound, that was the first thing I thought of," Palmer ruefully admitted. "But whether or not that site was intentionally chosen, what does the moving of the body suggest to you?"

"Well, that's simple. The murderer didn't want the body to be found at the scene of the crime."

"So?" Palmer encouraged.

"So, that would indicate that where he was killed was significant, or that the body would be found before the killer could get away, so he had to take him with him. Perhaps Stordahl was murdered in Fergus Falls, and the killer decided to make a getaway by going west to North Dakota or going to Canada, and if he had left the body where it was, there might have been that chance that it would have been found soon and we could have been after him far sooner."

Palmer sighed, "Well, yah, of course, but what else?"

"What do you mean?"

"If that was the case, why not keep the body a little longer—as long as you have it in the car anyway—and dump it in some obscure ditch in North Dakota where it might not be found for months?"

"Yeah, I can see that, but what are you getting at?"

"I think the body was moved so that we would not know where the murder took place. The killer did not want us to find the body there because it would automatically implicate him—or her, for that matter."

"You're not going to tell me that you think a woman could have done this?"

"Orly, Orly, Orly! You must keep all options open. That kind of thinking has derailed us more than once, if you remember. Frankly, the brutality of this makes it seem like a man's crime, but you gotta admit, Stover was a small man. A woman could have done it. But what I was getting at it is this: I think if we find out where the killing took place, we will find out who the killer was."

Orly nodded at this logic and said, "You might be right. But what do we do now?"

Palmer winced and said, "I've got to drive over to Battle Lake. While I'm gone, call up the Bureau of Criminal Apprehension in Bemidji. They might not be too happy that it's murder on Easter Sunday, but what can you do? Then make sure that you have secured the body for an autopsy. I suppose we will have to have a press conference to announce this, but that can wait until tomorrow. You can do some preliminary work for that while I'm gone. Clearly, we need to know more about the victim, so I suppose we will have to comb through Stordahl's apartment to see if there is anything that will give us any indication of who might have benefitted from his death. We can put that off until tomorrow as well. One thing we should do, however, is to see if there is anyone in Rothsay that can tell us anything. The night shift at the truck stop had all gone off work, and I didn't see any reason why we should have been in a hurry to question them. But they should be up and about by late afternoon, so why don't you drive back there and see if you can find anything out. Who's on duty this afternoon that might be free?"

"Well, there's Chuck Schultz. He's usually not busy. Of course, since the Twins game is on television, it would be a shame to take him away during duty hours."

The subject of Deputy Schultz always brought equal measures of pain and amusement to the two men. They had long ago given up trying to make a useful law enforcement officer out of him, but he did relate well with a certain segment of the county population, and was always just a little bit too valuable to fire. "Perhaps the game will be over by that time, and if it isn't, appease him with the promise that he can listen to it on your car radio. We wouldn't want to disturb him more than we have to. It is almost time for his annual idea."

KNUTSON EASED HIS ACURA in the direction of Battle Lake. This was not something to look forward to. He tried to divert his thoughts by selecting a CD of the Messiah. It usually inspired him, and he felt in desperate need of inspiration. He had missed Rolf's Easter service, after all. His brother always pulled out all the stops for Easter. He always found a couple of trumpeters to play "Thine is the Glory, Risen conquering Son," the stirring anthem from George F. Handel's *Judas Maccabaeus*. When Palmer was in college, he had taken part in the annual Christmas concert of the *Messiah*. He had been talked into this by a friend, but found that he loved it. He did not have the kind of voice that could handle, so to speak, the solos, but he could hit, with a lot of effort, the notes needed to sing second tenor, so he was a valued contributor. It was about this time that Rolf decided his church choir should sing it during Holy Week, and he asked Palmer to sing along, this time as a second bass, just because that was what they needed. Palmer may not have been ruby-throated, but he had range.

He could never resist singing along with the chorus, especially if he were alone in the car. Soon he was singing "And the glory, the glory of the Lord, shall be re -ve-e-e,-e-e e, e-e-eled." But then, he thought, "no, it isn't. Not when an innocent lamb like Stover can be murdered," and the miles passed as he wrestled with difficult theology.

The "Twilight Manor Retirement Home" was on the south shore of Battle Lake. It had been built in the late 1920s as a state-of-the-art resort that appealed to wealthy couples from Chicago and Minneapolis. It was completed in September of 1929. Needless to say, the potential vacationers who did not jump out of the window on Black Tuesday did not come the next summer. Prices were lowered, along with the amenities, as bankruptcies followed bankruptcies. By 1950, although the building was still in fine shape, it proved impossible to maintain as a luxury resort. It was at this time that it was resurrected as "Battle Lake Senior Home," but everybody called it the "old folks home." That quaint appellation stayed with the facility for the next thirty years until, under new management, it was decided that it was really a manor.

In any event, it served a valuable purpose. Most new "retirement centers" tended to cater to every need of the well-to-do. Twilight Manor catered to those who could not afford the luxuries, but needed a warm and safe place for their last days. In ages past, farms were taken over by the younger generation, and the grandparents had stayed on until they had joined the heavenly choir. But the young no longer returned to farms, and after a time it was impossible to live alone. Widows, widowers, and a few married couples found the manor by the lake to be a peaceful place for a final rest. In the summer, old men would drag a lawn chair out on the dock and do some fishing, sometimes putting bait on the hook and sometimes not. Out in the open air, they could sit and smoke forbidden cigarettes with a certain *joie d' vie* that thumbed their noses at science, authority, and bossy children. With the exception of an occasional jet ski driven by irrepressible teenagers, it was a quiet area of the lake—a place for contemplation and bird watching and squirrel feeding. There were always a few problems when it was time for the state inspection, but the obvious utility of the place and the evident love and attention shown to the residents, well, one just couldn't close it down and so it remained on a rather permanent conditional status.

It really was a rather nice day, Palmer thought as he parked his car. The dashboard thermometer told him that it was seventy-one degrees, clearly the warmest day yet in the year. He knew it wouldn't last, for already there were dark gray clouds to the west, and the fact that the ice on the lake had hardly started to melt reminded him that real spring was still a few weeks away. He breathed deeply and steeled himself for the unpleasant task ahead of him.

He passed through the rather elaborate gate and up to the porch with white pillars on either side. As he pushed open the front door, he smelled the familiar odor of "old." It seemed to hang from the light fixtures and billow up from the floor. It was the sort of smell one finds on large aluminum pots that don't ever seem to get clean no matter how much scrubbing is done. It was "institutional," with flowery cover-up scents over old perspiration and was so overly warm that he was on the point of gagging. And yet, as he looked into the dining room, a smell of fresh bread and roast beef carried with it a sense of nostalgia. He went to the front desk and asked to speak to the manager.

Sharon Busby was paged and came out of the dining room with a smile on her face. She recognized the sheriff, as most people in the county did, and greeted him warmly. And yet, the sunny face had given way to the wary face, for if the sheriff calls on Easter Sunday it is seldom good news. She was an attractive woman, with graying hair and rather oversized bifocals, and Knutson judged her to be about sixty years old. She introduced herself, shook his hand, and said, "And how can we help you?"

Palmer said, "I understand that you have a Joyce Stordahl working here. I need to have a word with her."

The manager said, "Yes, er, why don't you come into my office. Would you like a cup of coffee."

"Yes, that would be nice."

Sharon led the sheriff into the dining room and poured two cups of coffee. Knutson had expected the room to be gloomy and depressing. It was not. Instead it was a bright room decorated in yellow and white with decent quality artificial flowers and little baskets of Easter eggs on every table. There were a few people in wheel chairs, and at least one lady who was involved in an intense discussion with herself, but there were also lively conversations with children and grandchildren and, presumably, great-grandchildren. They brought their coffee back to Sharon's office.

With a directness that revealed her anxiety, Sharon Busby came to the point. "Joyce Stordahl has been living here for more than twenty years. She began working here only a year after I did, and has become a valuable employee and trusted friend. She is off duty today, but like most days, she is still on the grounds. I saw her down by the lake only about twenty minutes ago. I'll ask someone to go down to get her. But in the meantime, and I don't mean to pry, but I guess you wouldn't be here if it were not something serious, and I'd like to be prepared to help her if I could."

Palmer nodded and said, "I'm glad to hear that. Perhaps It will make my job a little easier. I'm afraid that I have to inform her that her son is dead."

Sharon gasped, muttered an "Oh, my God! John Stordahl!" and went to the door and called, "Jenny, would you go down to the lake and find Joyce and ask her to come to my office? . . . Yes, it is something serious, but try not to act like it, okay?"

Palmer waited until she was seated again and said, " Her son was killed sometime last night or early this morning. It is apparent that he was murdered. Someone found his body early this morning in Rothsay."

"In Rothsay. What would he be doing in Rothsay?"

"It appears that he was attacked somewhere else, and was just dumped in Rothsay. At this point, we know little more about it than that. Tell me, were you here when Stover, I mean John, came to live with his mother?"

"Yes, I was. We were worried about that at the time, but Joyce was needed here, and John didn't have anywhere else to go. We thought he could be useful in groundskeeping and maintenance, and so we agreed that he could stay in Joyce's small apartment. But, of course, it was not really an ideal place for a young man."

"Er, how did that work out, I mean, with his, er, disability and all?"

"Well, I have to admit that his occasional obscene outburst disturbed a lot of the old ladies at first. I mean, a few of the nice old Lutheran ladies had never heard such words. But I had a little talk with every one of them, and I convinced them that it was something that he just couldn't help, and after that, well, I guess they just kind of got used to him. I sometimes wonder if he didn't serve a purpose as a surrogate cusser—saying the words that they secretly wanted to say. In time, I believe that they all rather came to love him. But as I say, this is not the place for a young man. He would hang around the docks talking to the men, and he would go for a walk in the woods—I think he really missed his dog. In fact, he came to me with his idea of moving to Fergus Falls—he didn't want his mother to think he was abandoning her. I had a talk with Joyce about him. She was always very protective of him, and probably didn't give him the credit he deserved. In the end, the three of us found an apartment for him, and I know Joyce would generally go to see him at least every week or two. All in all, I thought the whole thing worked out rather well. But who would kill somebody like that? That's about the worst thing I've ever heard!"

"Yah," Palmer said slowly, "in my job you get to think you've seen it all. But this is just intolerable."

At this point, Joyce Stordahl came into the room. "What is it? Is it something about John? Jenny said not to worry, but she sure seemed to indicate it was something serious." At this point she noticed the uniformed sheriff and her voice lowered to a whisper. "It is serious, isn't it. And it's about John. What's happened to him?"

Palmer said, "Please sit down, Ms Stordahl. What I have to say is indeed serious." Palmer fell back on law enforcement legalese. "It is my duty to inform you that your son died sometime last night or early this morning. It appears that he was killed by a person or persons unknown. We have taken the body to the hospital in Fergus Falls. At some time, it need not be today, we will need you to make a formal identification."

Joyce Stordahl remained mute and straight in her chair, as if anxiously waiting for the sheriff to tell her that there might be some hope that the body may be that of someone else. The sheriff's next words destroyed that hope.

"It was my pleasure to get to know your son over the last month. I found him to be a sensitive person with a deep respect for nature. In the brief time I knew him, he spoke often of you, and I know that he loved you deeply. I shall miss him, as will many of the people he touched in the course of his life."

John's mother bravely held back tears and asked, "Can you tell me anymore about it?"

Knutson, feeling the worst was over, said, "A pair of motorists found his body near the statue of the prairie chicken at the Rothsay exit off Interstate 94 . . ."

"Rothsay! What was he doing there?"

"We don't think he was killed there. It appears he was attacked somewhere else and was dumped there later. (*My God*, thought Palmer, *couldn't I have used a more elegant expression than "dumped"?*) He had been struck on the back of his head by a blunt instrument, perhaps a pipe. I know that it's no consolation, but I don't believe he suffered much. At this point, we have no idea why this happened, or who could have committed this outrage. There's no hint that John ever, and I mean ever, had an enemy in the world."

Joyce Stordahl remained silent, nodding in the truth of Knutson's last statement.

"I understand you have good friends here,"— Sharon Busby put her arms around Joyce—"and I'm sure that they'll do everything that they can to comfort you in your loss. Rest assured that my office, and I personally, will do everything we can. I'll need to return to talk to you at a later date, to see if you can tell me anything about John's life that can provide us with an understanding as to how such a horror could have come to pass. I will leave you now, but please know that I share your sorrow."

The sheriff nodded and began to stand. Joyce Stordahl said simply, "Thank you, Sheriff. You've been most kind." Palmer let himself out and began walking to his car. "Well," he thought, "she took that well. What a brave woman!" At that point an inhuman wail came from inside Twilight Manor. It coldly echoed across the frozen lake. Palmer shivered.

Chapter Twelve

On Monday morning, Palmer and Ellie Knutson were "empty-nesters" again. Trygve had gotten a ride back to St. Olaf with his sisters, and the house was quiet. Palmer, showered and reasonably awake, stared into his closet. He decided that this was another day for him to wear his uniform, but since his trousers were reasonably clean, he merely opted for a clean shirt. After all, today he would have to face the media.

When he got to the courthouse, he discovered that Orly was already there, resplendent in his uniform as only a trim handsome young man could be. Palmer looked down sorrowfully at how the bottom two buttons on his shirt were spreading and sighed. He nodded as Orly got up to follow him into his office. Palmer stopped and got a cup of coffee. This was merely out of habit, since, spoiled by his own brew, he had grown to despise the pre-ground supermarket brand that the receptionist thought was adequate. He sat down, took an unconscious swig, and grimaced.

"So, Orly, what you got?"

Orly sat down and consulted his notes. "I was just in the process of typing up my report. You should have it in an hour. The bottom line is, I don't think I learned anything useful. As you suggested, I took Chuck along, and we went out to Rothsay late yesterday afternoon. It seems that there were four people on the night shift at the truck stop and Tesoro station. They had been working together for some time, knew each other pretty well, and could sort of vouch for each other. I'll put their names and telephone numbers in my report.

"Anyhow, we got lucky in that they were all home or at least nearby—well, a couple of 'em got rather nasty and said where else would they be since I was interrupting their supper. Bottom line is, none of them saw anything suspicious going on across the road. The guy selling gas, who seemed to be in charge of the night shift, said that activity in the middle of the night up by the prairie chicken really isn't as unusual as it would seem. He says he's seen couples up there in the summer at all hours of the night, kids drinking beer, travelers making car repairs, and stuff like that. He is pretty sure that he didn't see anything at all going on there on Saturday night, but admits even if he had he may not have paid much attention to it. The others, who are more inside and do not have the view out of the window that he does, pretty much said the same thing."

Palmer sucked his teeth and said, "Yah, that's about what I suspected. Still, when I hold that news conference at nine, I'm gonna appeal to anyone who might have stopped by there on Saturday night, who may have seen something, to give us a call."

"What do you want to do next, Sheriff?"

"I suppose we'd better go through Stover's apartment, see if we can find some notion why he was killed. Find out who owns that place—I presume he has a key—and have him meet us there at, oh, say 10:30. I rather dread going in there. The way he smoked, it must reek like an old time pool hall."

· ·

In THE PRESS CONFERENCE, the sheriff revealed to the assembled media all there was to report, which, he admitted, wasn't much. He told of the circumstances surrounding the discovery of the body, gave a brief biography of the victim and described the manner in which he had been killed. To the inevitable question of whether or not there were any suspects, Knutson merely replied that they were following various leads. At that answer, Orly looked up and blinked, but as he noticed that the sheriff was keeping a straight face, he reasoned that perhaps he knew something he had not been told. Knutson closed the conference by saying, "I had recently had the opportunity to get to know Mr. Stordahl, and I am grieved by his death. I shall do everything in my power to bring the perpetrator of this monstrous crime to justice."

A reporter for the Minneapolis *StarTribune* asked, "Does this mean that you'll be taking personal steps in this investigation?"

Palmer stared at him for a couple of seconds for dramatic effect and said, "You bet it does!"

THE SHERIFF AND HIS DEPUTY left for their appointment at Stover's apartment and in the car Orly asked, "What was that about 'various leads?' Do you really know something?"

"No," Palmer admitted. "Of course I don't. I would have told you if I did. But I'm quite sure the murderer is someone local. It doesn't hurt to make him—or her—a little nervous, does it?"

"Good point," Orly said, aware that he found himself learning his job more with every passing day.

It was a rotten day. The cold front had moved through overnight and a cold drizzle was being blown around by a sharp wind. In the brief time it took them to get to the car, Palmer was thoroughly chilled. He appreciated once again the seat warmers in his Acura as he pessimistically thought that yesterday would be the last nice day until May. April was such a tease!

They were met at the apartment of the late Stover Stordahl by Charles Radeck, a relatively young man who had rather quickly acquired rental property throughout the city. He was clearly anxious to help.

"This is the worst. Who would ever want to kill a guy like Stover. I mean, I didn't really know him very well. Actually, the only time I ever saw him was at the Flying Falcons games. He just sent in his rental check, regular as clockwork, never missed the first of the month. I could use more guys like him."

As he fumbled to find the right key, Palmer asked him, "When is the last time you were in here?"

"Huh? Well, I guess I've never been in here since I rented the place. Why?"

Palmer shrugged and said, "It's just that, you know, if you'd been in here recently, you may have been able to tell us if anything had changed. We're looking for just about anything that would tell us why Stover was murdered."

As the key was put in the door, Palmer and Orly took a deep breath and prepared for the worst. What they found was shocking. It was not a room discolored by nicotine stains on the ceiling. It was spotlessly clean, and smelling as fresh as a new house. Orly and Palmer looked at each other in surprise while the landlord exclaimed, "Wow, I sure won't have to do much to this place. It's nicer than when I rented it out."

Orly said, "But where are the ash trays? Where are the cigarette burns on the coffee table? Look at that clean carpet!"

Palmer asked Radeck to wait outside while they searched the apartment for any leads that would tell them about Stover's recent activities. Palmer, as usual, could not help but peruse the book case. "Look at this, Orly. It seems Stover was somewhat of a Civil War buff. Here's a whole section of Bruce Catton books. And here's stuff on World War I. And here, wow, look at this section on North American birds!" With sadness he looked at the birding book that was on the coffee table.

It was open to the section on the prairie chicken. Beside it was a notebook, with dates and locations for bird sightings, and an occasional sketch of a bird. The drawings were not without talent.

They put on latex gloves and began going through the life of the late Stover Stordahl. The kitchen table had a drawer that made it apparent that it had doubled as a desk. Inside were pay stubs from Fergus Falls State University, a balanced checkbook, a passbook savings account, pizza coupons, and various items one finds in a "junk drawer" when the owner prides himself on neatness. The refrigerator was filled with relatively healthy food, an almost full half gallon of milk, eggs, butter, and fruit. Certainly Stover had made no plans to leave.

Walking into the bedroom, Orly said, "Wow, look at this!" The walls of Stover's bedroom were covered with posters of the Minnesota Twins. Framed and under glass was a signed poster of Kirby Puckett saying, "To my pal Stover!!!!" Orly admired it reverently for a few seconds and said, "This guy grows in my estimation more every day."

The closet held very little in the way of clothes, and it was only here that evidence of Stover's great passion could be found. Wool, the apparent favorite in Stover's wardrobe, held the smell of tobacco very well.

"But no cigarettes. Don't you find this curious?"

It was then that Orly noticed a large cardboard box above a heating vent in the closet. He reached and pulled it down saying, "What do we have here?" Inside were fifty-three packages of Tareytons. "What do you suppose this is all about?" he asked the sheriff.

Palmer thought for a moment and said, "I think we are starting to get a look into the mind of Stover Stordahl. I had a brief conversation with his mother yesterday. She said she visited him every other week or so. I think it tells us one thing. Stover did not want to get caught smoking by his mother."

Palmer contemplated Stover's secret horde and said, "Do you remember those television commercials for Tareytons? They always showed somebody with a black eye and saying 'I'd rather fight than switch!'"

Orly furrowed his brow and said, "You mean, they actually used to advertize cigarettes on TV?"

Palmer couldn't believe what he was hearing. "You've never heard 'Winston tastes good like a cigarette should'? 'I'd walk a mile for a Camel'? 'Light up a Lucky'?' You really are disgustingly young."

Back in his office, after a short and unsatisfying lunch, Knutson made the call he had been dreading. He arranged to pick up Joyce Stover and bring her to Fergus Falls to identify the body and to interview her to find out more about her late son. Dr. Jimmy Clark, medical examiner, reported that a preliminary autopsy had been completed, and, as expected, showed that the cause of death was a massive brain injury inflicted by a blow to the back of the head. There was reason to believe, however, that the victim had not died immediately, but had probably been alive when he was dumped by the prairie chicken. Clark promised that the body would be cleaned up as well as possible, cheerily telling the sheriff that "All the damage was to the back of the head. The funeral parlor can get him looking pretty good for his mother. I expect we might have to ask her for permission to do a full autopsy, but she won't have to see the effects of that."

As he and Orly drove out of town, Palmer reflected that, if anything, the weather had only gotten worse. The outside thermometer reading on his dashboard read thirty-eight degrees, and he gloomily thought he detected a few flakes of snow in the air. After riding in silence for several miles, Orly said, "You know, I think they could have thought up a better name for a retirement center than 'Twilight Manor.' I mean, what does that say to you? 'Life is almost over. The darkness is coming. Prepare to go gentle into that dark night.' That's gotta be depressing. They could have just as well called it 'Waiting on God's Doorstep.' 'Last Bus Stop to Heaven.' 'Auditioning for the Choir Invisible.' "

Palmer joined in, "'Backstretch of the Last Mile,' 'Banana Peel before the Grave,' 'Saint Peter's Waiting Room.'" It was gallows humor, but it did put them in a better mood.

Joyce Stordahl was waiting for them as they entered Twilight Manor. She wore an appropriate black dress, the effect of which was somewhat diminished by a down coat necessitated by the harsh weather. The trip back to Fergus Falls was mostly in silence. At the hospital she identified her son and made arrangements with the funeral home to attend to his last needs. Palmer felt a surge of pride at the professionalism and concern in all the personel involved. It was already apparent that this murder had shocked the whole community.

Joyce Stordahl agreed to accompany the sheriff and his deputy back to his office. She accepted a cup of coffee and bravely faced the sheriff, knowing that this interview was both necessary and important.

"Now, as you indicated yesterday, John had lived in Fergus Falls for about twenty years, is that right?" Palmer asked.

"Yes, he moved directly here from our apartment at Twilight Manor."

"And has he lived at the same address since then?"

"Yes. He seemed to like it. It was close enough so that he could take his bike to the university, and close enough for him to walk downtown when he felt like it."

"Would you say he was happy there?"

"Oh, I suppose. As happy as he could ever really be, you know. He led a pretty lonely life, but I guess he got used to it."

"Did you see him often?"

"Probably about once a week. Generally he would find a way to come to visit me every two weeks, and I would usually come to Fergus Falls every other week. My main job at the retirement center, at least when I started, was as cleaning lady. I had all the supplies, you know, so I'd just stick them in my car and come over to his place and give it a good clean. Not that it needed much cleaning, John was always such a neat boy, er, man."

Palmer nodded, remembering the effect that the spotless apartment had made on him. He cleared his throat before saying, "I just need to get an understanding of his life. There seems no logical reason for his murder, and no one can think of a motive for this horrible crime. Perhaps if I knew more about his life, I'd be able to discover some pattern. Earlier in the day, we entered his apartment in search of clues to what he may have been doing in his last hours. Everything seemed to be in order. Tell me, was he interested in history? I saw several books on the Civil War, for instance."

"Well, I don't know. I suppose he was, a little, anyway. He talked about something he had seen of TV about the Civil War, so for his birthday I bought him a book about it. He seemed very thankful, so I bought him another one for Christmas. I kept this up for a while, but then I noticed that he hadn't really read them all. You must understand, there was nothing mentally wrong with John. But that doesn't mean that he would ever have been a very good student. He liked history, but I think mainly he liked to watch the history channel. Reading books? Well, he did read, but not all that much, I guess. He did love his bird books, though, and lately I have been buying some of those. I've been able to take him up to that big Barnes and Noble store in Fargo. We used to get a cup of coffee there and he'd sit with several bird books and then pick out the one he wanted . . ." Joyce stopped talking and wiped a tear from her eye. "Excuse me, Sheriff," she said softly.

Palmer waited for a while and gently asked, "Did he have anyone that he regularly, you know, er, did things with?"

Joyce Stordahl thought for a while, and finally said, "No, I couldn't really say he did. He was generally quite lonely, I suppose. Curiously, he mentioned you the last time that I talked to him. He was looking forward to the trip to see the prairie chickens. Tell me, did he seem happy that day?"

The sheriff remembered with horror the last few minutes of the prairie chicken fiasco, especially with Roxanne Dahl screaming at Stover and then turning a chicken into road kill, but said, "Yes, he really seemed to enjoy being out there." Which was, of course true, if one were to ignore the unhappy last few moments. "Did he have any other hobbies?"

"He sure liked the Minnesota Twins, I can tell you that. He used to watch the Vikings, but they just, well, they just upset him too much. But he could tell you everything the Twins have done for the last twenty years. Other than that, oh, I don't know, he liked to smoke, of course, but I wasn't supposed to know about that. He also just seemed to like Fergus Falls. He told me that sometimes, just before he went to bed, summer or winter, he liked to take a walk around town. He said it was always so peaceful. As he put it, 'Everybody just watches the ten o'clock news and goes to bed. I kind of like to walk around downtown and see that everything is all right for the night.' Does that surprise you?"

Palmer thought for a while and replied, "No, I don't think it does. If I'm out late and go through downtown, I feel sort of the same way. Well, we won't keep you any longer. If you need anything, or if you want to spend some time in John's apartment, or if you need to do any shopping, we're at your disposal. Whenever you are ready, we can take you back to Twilight Manor. And if you can think of anything, anything that may not seem important but is in any way out of the usual, give us a call—day or night."

"Thank you, Sheriff. I think I would like to go by his apartment. I have a key, and I will see if I can find anything out of the ordinary. He did keep it pretty neat, as you noticed, so if anything is significantly disturbed, I would probably be able to tell. Sharon Busby, at the Manor, has been so helpful and I don't know what else I should do about funeral arrangements. I've decided that he should be buried in Fergus Falls—anyplace else would be unthinkable. John didn't go to church all that often, I guess, but I want to talk thinks over with that old guy at the big Lutheran church. Do you know him?"

"Yah, he's my brother?"

"Oh, really. Er, do you think it will be possible to have the funeral there?"

"Knowing Rolf, Yah, I'm sure he'll be most eager to help in any way he can. Meanwhile, I'm going to ask one of my deputies, Chuck Schultz, to be your chauffeur for the rest of the day. It is so nasty outside, I don't want to have you walk anywhere. Just tell him when and where you want to go."

As Joyce rose, Palmer and Orly both stood. Palmer came around and took both of her hands and said, "Thank you for your help, and again, accept our sympathy on your loss. Orly, go get Chuck."

After she had gone, Palmer looked at Orly and said, "I think we just learned something there. If Stover had taken one of his nightly walks to put the town to bed, it was his last walk. Which means, he maybe saw something, or somebody doing something, that he was not meant to see. The big question is, 'what?'"

CHAPTER THIRTEEN

ALMER KNUTSON HAD SPENT A RESTLESS NIGHT. Unable to sleep, he had tried to think of some direction for the investigation. Responding to his call at the press conference for anyone having seen Stover Stordahl on Saturday night to call the Sheriff's Office, someone had reported that they had seen him downtown at about 11:30, shuffling down Lincoln Avenue. "All right, so he was alive at that time. Then what? What should be done next?"

He awoke several times during the night, and that question was always in the forefront of his mind.

After an hour of semi-consciousness, he awoke at seven and went into his daughter's unused room. He had turned it into what he liked to call his 'spa.' He turned his radio on to Minnesota Public Radio and, hoping to hear some energetic Beethoven, he climbed onto his Nordic Trak. By and large, he hated to exercise, but the music and the rhythm of the skis helped the time pass. After a savage workout, the most he had done in weeks, he showered and went down to breakfast.

Ellie had surprised him by making a cheese, ham, and green pepper omelet. It was a favorite. He leaned forward and kissed his wife over the breakfast table and sat down to attack it with gusto, only briefly reflecting that he was essentially undoing all the calorie burning he had done on the Nordic Trak. He was spreading his second English muffin with strawberry jam when Ellie asked, "So, what are you going to do today?"

Palmer replied, "I think I have to learn more about Stover. We know that he spent his days at the university field house, for instance. Now I really don't think there is any connection to the university. Because of the senseless nature of the crime, someone suggested a 'thrill killing.' I mean, ever since Leopold and Loeb, back in the 1920s, people start thinking that maybe a couple of college kids murdered someone just for kicks. The more I do this job, the more aware I become that anything, no matter how unlikely, can happen. But I really doubt there is any campus connection. Still, I want to find out more about the victim, and that would seem to indicate that I should go to those people who saw him on a regular basis. So, I think I'll go up to the university and talk to the people at the fieldhouse where Stover worked. Can I get you more coffee?"

"Yah, as long as you're up." Ellie leaned back and thoughtfully smeared just a little more butter on her toast. "You know, I was thinking about all that tension you were talking about last week. The conservationists didn't shoot the hunters and the hunters didn't shoot the developers, and now, it seems, all over town, people want to come together to find out who killed Stover. But still, you know, your first instincts may have been right. Maybe Stover didn't see something, maybe he knew something. He'd been taking those walks around town for a long time, and maybe he didn't even realize the significance of what he knew. But someone thought he did, and was just waiting for him to begin his walk on a dark Saturday night. By the way, today is that big funeral for Aldwin Monson. I suppose your brother will do the service."

"Yah," Palmer agreed, "I'd forgotten about him. Did I tell you that Joyce Stordahl said she was going to ask Rolf to do Stover's funeral? He's in for a busy week."

Ellie leaned back with her cup and said, "Have you heard anything about what will happen to the bank? As I understand it, Monson had some pretty big plans for expansion and had bought up almost the whole block for development. I wonder if that'll go forward."

Palmer, somewhat disinterested in the future of banking at the moment, said, "I imagine it will. I suppose his wife inherits the estate, of course, but I think that she was also a bank director. And he had guys as vice-presidents who'd been with him for a long time. I shouldn't think there will be much change. Besides, if that bank's going to continue to be the development engine behind that ethanol plant, well, I'm sure your old friend Congressman Paulson and his cronies will see that it goes through. I suppose he might even be at the funeral—the second time in a year that he actually sets foot in Fergus Falls. Are you going to stalk him?"

"At a funeral? Yah, that'd look nice, wouldn't it? But who knows, maybe he'll look up and see your brother in all his glorious raiment and repent of his sins. I mean, every time I see him, I'm ready to confess to sins I haven't yet considered committing. Who else are you going to see?"

"Good question. Where to begin? It seems Stover was really into birds. Maybe I should look into that a little more. You know more about that bird watching society than I do. What was Stover like at meetings? I presume there weren't a whole lot of birds to watch in the winter."

"You'd be surprised. More than you think. But really, I just went to one meeting before the one I dragged you to. You really ought to talk to Carolyn Dahl." Ellie sighed, "She's so pretty."

"Who? Carolyn Dahl?"

"Of course. And don't tell me you hadn't noticed. Beautiful skin. She can afford to have her hair done whenever she wants to. I don't know if she has had an eye job or not, but mine haven't looked that good in ten years. She's almost four years older than I am, and she still has that disgusting girlish figure. But anyway, I suppose she would be someone to talk to."

Palmer smiled and got ready to go to the office. It was still brutally cold, so he decided in favor of his deep blue Norwegian sweater with the pewter buttons instead of his uniform. Heated seats or not, it was still a cold drive to the courthouse.

In his office, he took the opportunity to have another cup of coffee, which was, if anything, worse than yesterday's. In fact, he considered, maybe it was yesterday's. The Tuesday *New York Times* crossword puzzle was ridiculously easy. With no other excuse for delay, he called the university and made an appointment with Lamont Miller, the university athletic director and overall head of the fieldhouse. He checked with Orly to see if there had been any tips or information on Stover's activities and then the two of them made their way to the university.

The university had changed dramatically since Palmer had attended in the 1960s. As they walked past Mickelson Hall, he remembered his first year in college. It had been a relatively new freshmen boy's dorm then. The girl's dorms were on the other side of the campus. The girls had hours, the boys did not. The boys could smoke in their rooms, the girls could not. There was one day in the fall, the Saturday of parent's weekend, when all of the dorms were open, and boys could enter and visit girls in their room, so long as the door was kept open. To the boys of Fergus Falls State Teacher's College, as it was called then, entering into that forbidden territory was more exotic than going to Tibet. And now Mickelson Hall was coed. Women and Men, no longer boys and girls, were on alternate floors and there was no demilitarized zone between them. There seemed to be a general agreement that the men shouldn't enter the women's shower room, but that seemed to be the only proscription.

If the boys of the 1960s had pulled a Rip Van Winkle and awakened in a dorm in the twenty-first century, they would have thought they had died and gone to heaven. Every room was stocked with computers, DVD players, televisions, audio reproduction elements (a stereo? What was that?) carpeting, and private phones. And only a few feet away there were women. Palmer sighed.

Palmer and Orly made their way to the Fjelde Fieldhouse and were directed to the plush offices of the athletic director. A receptionist offered coffee and, of course, both accepted. It was Palmer's fourth cup of the morning, but was probably even better than his brew. She led them into a room featuring deep green carpeting and a large abstract diptych. Palmer, who had learned a thing or two about art from Ellie, recognized by the fantastic colors that it was a recent work of a prominent local artist named Thill. An extremely large man rose from his desk to greet them. "Hi, I'm Lamont Miller. Glad to meet you."

Palmer responded, "I'm Palmer Knutson, and this is my Chief Deputy, Orly Peterson."

Orly, in fact, could not take his eyes off of him. He had noticed him in town before, because there can hardly be anyone more noticeable than a six-foot-nine black man in a small city in western Minnesota. But it was more than that. Up close, Miller seemed to have an aura about him. Orly had expected a booming voice such as that of James Earl Jones, but instead found the soft, rather high, voice even more commanding. Orly spilled some coffee on his pants.

Miller said, "Yes, I've seen you on TV. In fact, I think I've seen your wife on TV too. She is some sort of activist, isn't she?"

Knutson, proud and embarrassed at the same time, said, "Er, yes, I guess you could say so."

"Good for her, good for her. Now, how can I help you today?"

The sheriff said, "As you no doubt know, one of your employees was murdered over the weekend. We are trying to get as much information on the victim as we can so we can piece together his life. As it is, no one seems to know all that much about Stover Stordahl. We'd like to know about his job, how he related to his fellow workers, and how he related to the university. I guess I really don't know what I'm looking for at this point, but we have to start somewhere. Is there anything you can tell us about him?"

Miller looked pained for a few seconds, and then leaned back and a smile gradually came over his face. The smile became a grin, and a warm chuckle came from several feet down in his body. "Stover, Stover, Stover. That's all anybody's been talking about around here since we heard the news. We were devastated. But the thing is, I sort of got the feeling that as I talked to people around the fieldhouse, everyone thought he was someone else's friend. It's kind of hard to explain. Everyone liked him. He did his job well. As the chief custodian said, 'He always did exactly what you told him to do.' Now, maybe he didn't have the most initiative to do what you hadn't told him to do, but everybody liked him. There would be times when there was some little celebration going on and everyone would be there except Stover. It turned out that everyone just assumed that someone else would tell him. It'd make everyone feel rotten, of course, but it'd happen again and again."

Knutson asked, "Did you yourself have any relationship with him?"

Miller nodded and said, "You know, that's one of the things that makes his death hard to deal with. It's like we all had a relationship with him, but we never took it seriously. I mean, he was a little guy and, as you may have noticed, I'm not. Stover seemed kind of in awe about that, so I tried to put him at ease. I told him that he could call me 'High Pockets' and I'd call him 'Low Pockets.' Every time I saw him I called out, 'Hey there, Low Pockets,' and he'd chirp back 'Hi, Mr. High Pockets.' Of course, the students heard that. I became Mr. High Pockets overnight, but they'd never call me that to my face. And yet, you know, that is practically the only communication we ever had. I feel bad about that. And, it seems, others around here feel the same way.

"And then there were the students. They really liked him. Of course, sometimes I think they liked him especially when they could talk him into doing something. I don't know whether or not you heard about this—indeed, we did our best to keep it quiet—but one of the dorms organized a skinny dipping party at the pool. They found out what night Stover was on night duty, and persuaded him to leave the door to the pool open. Imagine the law suits something like that could cause! In any event, if there had been law suits, those would have been the only suits associated with the adventure. Curiously, nobody found out it about until about a month later, when someone just couldn't help bragging, but I don't think we ever really found out who organized it. I suppose it doesn't much matter anyhow. But Stover, well, apparently that group of students just couldn't do enough for him after that.

"You can tell that now, today, on campus. There are plans for a Stover Stordahl memorial service. I mean, we're behind it, of course, but the real driving force for it is coming from the students. It's a shame, really, that none of us—staff, faculty, or students—never really took the trouble to show him that he was a special person while he was alive. It makes you want to reassess things. For the first time, I suppose, I told my secretary this morning how much she means to me."

Knutson then asked him, "How long have you been athletic director here?"

"I came seven years ago in the position of 'Assistant Athletic Director.' I was one of President Gherkin's 'star hires.' Of course, he merely wanted a black person on the staff so he would look better down in St. Paul. A week after I was hired, the Athletic Director got drunk, fell out of his boat and drowned. Gherkin never had any real intention of giving me any responsibilities, but suddenly I was his acting A.D. He also figured that if he got an ex-NBA player it would help in recruiting. He wasn't really wrong there. Since I came we have been able to entice some top notch talent to the program, as evidenced by the championship teams we have had lately. Of course, most of that credit would have to go to the kids and the coach. Gherkin had his own pet candidate for the coaching position, and he thought he could force him down my throat. That was the showdown with him, and I knew it. He thought he'd merely found a house slave. But after six years playing for the Golden State Warriors, I'd saved my money and had always planned to go back to get my Ph.D. in athletic administration. I got a former NBA assistant coach to head up our program and haven't looked back since. The last six years have been sweet, and I'm going to miss the Fergus Falls Flying Falcons."

Orly Peterson, in awe of being in the presence of a one time professional basketball player, blurted out, "Does this mean you're leaving."

"Yes I am. I was going to announce it this week, but with the murder of Stover and all, I've decided to announce it next Monday. I have been hired as the athletic director of Michigan State University."

"Wow," said Orly Peterson. "The Spartans! Good for you! But the university is sure going to miss you."

"Oh, I don't know. I think I'm leaving it in pretty good shape," he replied, his pride evident in every word.

"Yah, well," Palmer cut in. "Let me offer my congratulations as well. Meanwhile, if you hear of anything on campus, any connection, however remote, give us a call."

"I'll do that sheriff. I want to see you get this man. We all do. And I'll tell you something else. If there is any student on this campus who finds out anything, you can be sure he'll tell you. They might not always like cops, but in this case, we're all in it together."

As they walked out of the building and passed the cavernous basketball arena, Palmer wistfully remembered playing intramural basketball in the old gym. It seemed like a hundred years ago.

Orly said, "What's next?"

Palmer conscientiously picked up a beer can and tossed it in the recycling bin. "I thought we'd have a talk with Carolyn Dahl. She's head of the Otter Tail County Birdwatching and Conservation Society, and that was the last acknowledged event involving Stover. I called her earlier and left a message. Hold on," (Palmer, unused to cell phones, now remembered that he carried one) "let me see if she's gotten back to me." After two or three attempts to access his voice mail, accompanied by a mild expletive and a muffled Orly snicker, he discovered that Mrs. Dahl had invited him to come to her home at 1:00, if that would be convenient.

"Okay, so, maybe we should have lunch first. Where do you want to go?"

Orly shrugged, "Maybe we could eat on campus."

"At Ptomaine Hall? I barely survived four years of that stuff. We can do better than that."

"Then how about either Taco Bell, Subway, or Burger King?" Orly suggested.

"Yah, that's better. They're all fine with me. Which one do you want?"

"Actually," Orly said with an air of supercili-ousness, "that's why I suggested eating on campus. The new food service has all three. I can have a taco, you can have a burger."

Knutson just shook his head. "Amazing."

Chapter Fourteen

T HE SHERIFF GUIDED HIS ACURA into the driveway of a magnificent dwelling on the shores of Lake Alice. Above the front door was a conspicuous wooden sign reading "The Dahl House." He thought, on consideration, that it was an appropriate name, since it looked like one of those metal doll houses that his daughters used to play with. Everything was extremely tidy, with a full bed of tulips and daffodils heralding the arrival of spring. The front door was framed with white pillars and the windows were framed with white shutters. "How can this house look so clean after a winter like we just had?" Knutson thought, picturing the spring work he needed to do on his house. Carolyn Dahl answered the doorbell on the first ring and graciously invited them into the house. She took their coats and ushered them into the living room.

Knutson noticed two things. First, this was no ordinary living room. A baby grand piano occupied the far side of the room, while a lovely stone fireplace silently purred with a gas fire. They were soon seated on deep sofas covered with soft leather. On the glass and steel coffee table, a thermos carafe and a tray of Pepperidge Farm cookies awaited them.

The other thing Knutson noticed was that Ellie was right. Carolyn really was a beautiful woman. He had not noticed before, because to Palmer, there was only one ultra-beautiful woman on the planet, and that was Ellie. But as he studied Carolyn, he noticed that she wore an Italian wool sweater and a welcoming smile, and well, she was no Ellie, of course, but she was a looker. She asked, "Would you care for some coffee?"

There are clichés that tend to be exaggerated, such as a "knee-jerk reaction." But just as the human body can't keep itself from kicking the foot when tapped below the knee, Palmer said, "Of course, that'd be wonderful." As he said it, he realized that he should have declined, but, now, of course, oh well. He received the cup and took a cautious if guilty sip. "My gosh," he thought, "this is even better than what I had at the athletic director's office. Maybe my homemade coffee isn't so good after all." But it was time to get down to the business at hand.

"I suppose you are wondering why I want to talk to you about Stover Stordahl. Well, I appreciate that you may not be able to tell us anything that would help in finding out who murdered him, but I'm just trying to get hold of his character. I know that he was very active in the Otter Tail County Bird Watching and Conservation Society, and that you were along on that outing on the last day of his life. Would he, perchance, have said anything to you that, looking back on it, indicated that he felt at all worried or threatened?"

Carolyn Dahl thought for a minute and said, "You know, I've asked myself that question ever since I heard about his death. That day, at least until the unpleasantness caused by my daughter, I thought he was about as happy as I'd ever seen him. There was no indication that he had a care in the world, as far as I could see. But then, I really didn't know him well."

"How long had he been a member of your group?"

"We've been in existence for less than a year. I seem to remember he was at the first meeting. But, then, I suppose, he wasn't the kind of person one got to know well. He was always willing to help—he'd volunteer to do almost anything needing doing. It's just that, I don't quite know how to say this, but he wasn't really the type of person that, um, the type of person one wanted as a leading, um, well, face of the organization. I tried to get some interest in going down to St. Paul to lobby for conservation issues. He was the first person to volunteer. But I mean, it would probably not advance the cause of conservation to have a person get excited and blurt out an obscenity before a senate committee now, would it?"

Knutson sighed and said, "I suppose not."

"But I can hear the censure in your voice. The reaction of the community ever since he was killed has been sort of a 'good old Stover. What a fine guy.' And he was, I suppose, but none of us ever went beyond that. You, yourself, for instance—I'd guess your only real conversation with him was last Saturday when we went birdwatching."

Knutson ruefully admitted that was true.

"Now that he's gone, I suppose we all wish we had listened and taken him a bit more seriously. But we didn't, and however much we may regret this, it is just the way it was. I was far more concerned about our hopes of getting a nature preserve from old Homer Grimstead. And now, apparently, that isn't even going to happen. Do you know anything more about that?"

Palmer said, "No, I guess I don't. The only time I ever heard about it was at your meeting last month, when you indicated that you had hopes for such a thing. But Homer just died last week, you know, so maybe they haven't gotten around to dealing with his estate yet. That can take some time, you know."

"In fact, my daughter had a date with Jack Grimstead—Homer's nephew—just last Saturday night. She asked him about it. He said it was something his uncle mentioned once or twice, but he also told him he was going to give it to some hunting club. That's ironic, don't you think? One society wants to protect wildlife; the other wants to blast it to kingdom come. But he said that, although his uncle had talked about it, he had never actually made it official. I suppose he inherits, but I don't know if he intends to honor his uncle's wishes—whatever they might have been."

It seemed that they were straying from the goal of finding out more about Stordahl, and Palmer looked for a way to get back to the subject. He said, "So your daughter—Roxanne, is it?—was out on Saturday night? Perhaps she may have seen something. Is she at home?"

Carolyn let out a suffering sigh and said, "Yes, as usual, she's home. I'll go and get her."

As she left the room, Orly looked at Palmer and Palmer looked at Orly and both simultaneously reached for another cookie. Carolyn soon appeared leading an obviously unwilling daughter dressed in a sweat suit. Her hair was a mess, she wore no makeup, and she had a cord from an ipod hanging around her neck. It was apparent to Orly, however, that she had not been working out, even though, he thought unkindly, she certainly needed to. To say she snarled would indicate that she cared enough to have an attitude about her guests. Instead, if such a condition can be said to exist, she whined with hostility. "Yeah, what do you want me for?"

We don't! thought Orly. But the sheriff said, "We understand you were out on Saturday night. Did you go downtown, and, if so, did you see Stover Stordahl or anything at all unusual?"

"Yes, I was downtown and, no, I didn't see any-thing unusual and, no, I didn't see that little creep Stover Stordahl."

Palmer tried his best to keep the revulsion out of his voice. "And you were with Jack Grimstead? Where did you go?"

"Yeah, I went out with Jack. Mother says I should try to get out more. I went into Nora's Knitting Nook a couple of weeks ago, and there he was. I'd never seen him before, but he said he had just bought the business and would give me a good deal on anything I wanted. And he did. So we got to talking, and last week he called me up and asked me out. I didn't have anything better to do. He took me to the Blue Fox."

Palmer, overcompensating for his innate hostility, said, "Oh, did you have a nice time?"

"What's it to you?"

"Just asking. People have said the food there is quite good."

"It was okay, I suppose."

"I asked your mother this, but she was unable to provide any insight. That trip out to the nature preserve was the last time that many people saw Stover Stordahl alive. Did he say anything, or did you observe anything that may have led you to believe that he might have been in danger?"

"No. But what would I know? I'd never seen him before. I didn't know he had Tourette's syndrome— Thanks a lot, Mother!—so I suppose I was not overly 'sensitive' (In using this word, she composed her fingers into quotation marks)."

That's putting it mildly, thought Palmer.

"So, no, I didn't notice anything, did I!"

"What time did you get home from your date?" Palmer inquired.

"'What time did you get home from your date?' You sound like my father whenever he used to grill me."

"I'm merely asking so that we can establish some time frame. If you were home before the last time Stover was sighted, then we can be assured that nothing out of the ordinary occurred when you were downtown."

"Oh, yeah, okay. I thought Jack was planning to make a night of it, but after coffee and a brandy, during which time he did nothing but gloat about some big real estate deal he was working on, he took me right home."

I'll bet he did, thought both the sheriff and his deputy. Out loud, Palmer asked, "And what time was that?"

"About ten-thirty. I got home in time to watch most of *Saturday Night Live.* It was stupid."

"Your date?"

"Well, maybe that, too, but I was talking about *Saturday Night Live.*"

At this point, Orly surprised Palmer by bluntly stating: "But you didn't stay home, did you! Didn't you go out again?"

Roxanne snarled, "So how come you know so much about my business? Yeah, I was, like, all dressed up and nowhere to go. I hardly expected to be dumped off so early! There was going to be live music at the Blue Fox, but could we stay for that? Noooo. So I thought, 'There's no reason why I can't go by myself. Maybe I'll meet somebody more interesting than Jack Grimstead. You got a problem with that?"

Palmer intervened to say, "No, of course not. But I can't help but wonder, however, why you didn't volunteer that information earlier."

150

"Because it's none of your business, that's why!"

"Miss Dahl, in a murder investigation, everything is our business. Did anyone see you there?"

"Yeah, I guess you could say so. There was this guy sitting all by himself and I thought, 'Hey, he looks about my age' and he was alone and so I went to his table and sat with him."

"What was his name?"

"You are nosy, aren't you? I don't remember, but he said he was some kind of aide to that smarmy congressman."

"Was it Chadd Hangar?"

"Yeah, I think that was it. So I'm talking to him for a while and it became very apparent that he wasn't interested. It turns out he doesn't like girls, if you know what I mean. What an awful night!"

Orly asked, "And while you were downtown then, did you see anything of Stover Stordahl?"

"Weren't you listening before? I told you I hadn't seen him again."

Talking to Mrs. Dahl had been pleasant enough, but there's only so much citizens can expect from their elected officials, and speaking to Roxanne Dahl for an extended time was going above and beyond the call of duty. Besides, it was apparent that nothing more of interest could be gained. Palmer and Orly graciously thanked Roxanne and her mother and left.

In the car, Knutson asked, "What made you ask if she had gone out again? That was brilliant!"

Orly was pleased. "I don't know. I'd never met her before, so maybe I was imagining things, but she looked nervous. But it makes you think, though, doesn't it. She was probably downtown when Stordahl got whacked."

"And so, it would seem, was Chadd Hangar," Palmer added.

IN A QUIET, RESIDENTIAL PART OF TOWN, three sixth grade boys had created their own secret Tuesday Club. There were only two rules to the club: "Tell No One!" and "No girls!" The second rule was a matter of principle and preference. The first rule was a matter of necessity. This was made of utmost importance by the location of the club. The Otter Tail River was only a block from the homes of the three boys. All three sets of parents had made it a rule ever since the boys could walk that there was to be no playing by the river. But one day last summer, Aaron Smemo had discovered that, in a bend of the river, erosion had created a nook in the earth that resembled a shallow cave. In front of this indentation, there had grown up concealing underbrush. It was, the boys believed, the most concealed place in town. Perfect for a clubhouse. So far, there were only three members, but they had just about decided to expand membership to include the new kid in the neighborhood.

After school, Aaron told his mother that he was going to Johnny MacLarnan's house, Johnny told his mother that he was going to Kyle Mattson's house, and

Kyle had told his mother that he was going to Aaron's house. It was perfect. They were all going to the clubhouse. To be sure, the leaves hadn't come out on the bushes yet, but it was still well concealed. For Aaron's purposes, it had to be. One by one they made their way to their inner sanctum.

When they were all present, Aaron took one final look out of the "cave" and said, "Look what I've got!"

He reached inside his jeans, then fumbled around inside his underwear and produced an almost complete package of cigarettes. "Care for a smoke?" he said, trying to sound nonchalant.

Kyle and Johnny looked at him with a mixture of fear and suspicion. They had remembered the public service announcements on television that said that if a friend offered you a cigarette, he was not really your friend. But, on the other hand, Aaron was a friend. He was a member of the Tuesday Club. Aaron coyly appropriated the motto of Las Vegas that he had heard on television, and said, "What happens in the Tuesday Club, stays in the Tuesday Club."

Johnny, hoping against hope, said, "You got any matches?"

"No," Aaron said, "my parents won't let me play with matches. But nobody said I couldn't use one of these." He pulled out a device for lighting charcoal which he had stuck in his jacket pocket.

"Ooh, cool," said little Kyle Mattson.

"Where did you get these?" Johnny asked.

"So, on Sunday morning, see, I have to go downtown to where I pick up the papers for my paper route. I saw 'em lying on the sidewalk. I figgered the pack was empty, so I gave it a kick. But, as you can see, it was almost full. I thought it would be a shame to waste 'em."

Needless to say, the Great Tuesday Club Smoker was not a success. There were a couple accidental inhalations, some coughing, and for the most part more blowing through than sucking on the cigarette occurred. Nevertheless, while each one felt slightly nauseous, they all agreed it had been a fine thing to do. Aaron pried a rock out of the bank and said, "And here is where we will keep them, so that at any time when one of us feels like he 'needs a smoke,' he can come down here and light up." And now that they all had a great secret, the Tuesday Club was a more tightly bound brotherhood.

Chapter Fifteen

BEFITTING THE CHANGING NATURE of Minnesota weather, the next day dawned bright and sunny, and the breeze from the south seemed to indicate some promise of spring. This put Sheriff Knutson in an extraordinarily good mood. He had enjoyed a good night's sleep and in the morning had experimented with his coffee mixture and had decided that it was more like that which he had enjoyed the day before. As he moseyed up the steps of the Court House, he met Stacie Ryan, reporter for the *Daily Journal*, coming down.

"Good Morning, Sheriff, I was hoping I'd run into you. I just stopped by your office to see if you had anything you could tell me concerning your investigations into the death of Stover Stordahl. The whole town's talking about it, and since it's his funeral today, which promises to be quite the affair, I just wanted to be kept up to date."

"Er, hi Stacie. Um, I really don't have much to tell you. When I've got something to announce, I'll let you know."

A good reporter would not be put off so easily. "There's a lot of speculation going around about why anyone would do such a thing. Why kill him? Some people think it may be a 'thrill killing' or that this was the work of a serial killer. Any reaction?"

Palmer felt guilty enough about having no leads or indeed any particular direction to follow in the investigation. He was starting to get a bit defensive about it. "No," he said, "I'm quite sure it isn't anything like that."

"So you do have some suspicions. What can you share with us?"

"As I've said, I don't have anything to share with you at this time."

"Does that mean you do not have any suspects?"

More to get rid of her than anything else, Palmer said, "I didn't say that. I have a real good idea about who is behind this, but I'm keeping that information to myself. I don't want any of the innocent parties that may be connected with this investigation to be subject to rumor or innuendo. Now, if you'll excuse me, I must get back to my deputies to discuss the case."

As Palmer hurried up the stairs, Ryan shrugged and thought to herself, *Well, he didn't say that was off the record. This could be my big opportunity. If my story gets picked up by the major papers, this could be my chance for the big time.*

THE SHERIFF ENTERED HIS OFFICE, took off his jacket, got a cup of horrible coffee, and sat at his desk. He was trying to think of what to do next, and, until he did, well, the *New York Times* crossword puzzle beckoned. As he was trying to remember the "periodic chart of elements" from his high school chemistry class, to fill in the squares that asked for the abbreviation for copper, Orly entered.

"Morning, Chief!"

"Don't call me 'Chief.'"

"Good morning, Sheriff,"

"That's better."

"What's on tap for today?"

"You got any suggestions?"

"Not really," the deputy admitted, "but I thought I might make sort of a chart. One that'd have a timeline for when we know Stover was last sighted, where that was, times that he usually went out walking at night, if we can determine that, and other people who roam around town at that time of night who might have seen him, etc., you know, to see if there is any pattern or any suggestion of where we can take this investigation. Someone once told me that it sometimes helped to get it all down, and in that concentration, the way might be prepared for inspiration."

"Who told you that load of b.s?"

"You did."

"Oh. Well, go do it then."

Palmer returned to his puzzle, but it was impossible to concentrate. He tried to think of who else he should talk to, but then reasoned that the funeral would be that afternoon. In the first place, many of the people he really should talk to would be there, and in the second place, it was not unheard of for the murderer to show up for his victim's official sendoff. Unlikely, of course, but then, he really didn't have any other direction. Meanwhile, there were other things to attend to. He looked at his "in box" where he kept loose notes to himself. On the top was sheet of paper that said simply, "file for reelection?????" He moved it to the bottom of the pile.

IN MANY WAYS, THE FUNERAL for Stover Stordahl was one of the oddest he had ever attended. The huge Lutheran church was filled to the balcony. As Palmer sat there and joined in the singing, he couldn't help but wonder how many in this congregation ever knew who Stover Stordahl really was, or, for that matter, would really miss him now that he had gone. Palmer admitted that he hadn't known the man well either, yet he was there. There were a couple of hundred college students, mainly in the back and in the balcony. Cynically, Palmer wondered how deep was their sorrow, and how joyous their opportunity to go out and do something different. But then, Stover was almost a mascot for the university athletic teams, and his presence would certainly be missed, at least for a year or two. The staff of the fieldhouse was all there, led in by Lamont Miller, who was, naturally, noticed by everyone. Palmer also suspected that many in the audience were simply drawn by a goulish desire to see the funeral of a murder victim. Murder has always had a macabre lure on the human psyche, and, Palmer suspected, the citizens of Fergus Falls were no different than anyone else in that regard.

Joyce Stordahl was there, bearing up bravely and looking pleased but perhaps a little awed at the size of the crowd. Palmer always thought that his brother Rolf did funerals better than any clergyman in the state, and the Reverend Knutson did not disappoint on this occasion. He spoke of a mother's love, and determinedly dry eyes became misty. He talked about duty and the love of the university, and the students almost cheered. Finally, he spoke about acceptance and tolerance for all of God's children, and everyone felt guilty. *Yup*, Palmer thought, *Rolf's done it again.*

The crowd filed out, nodded to each other, and went down to the basement for the required light lunch prepared by the Ladies Aid. The sheriff mingled, gave his sympathy to the bereaved yet again, and itched to leave. Yet, these were the citizens he was sworn to protect, and he hoped that as their sheriff, decked out in his best uniform, he would be a calming presence, a mooring stone in the midst of a storm of people absurdly wondering if the murderer would strike again. To every anxious inquiry about the progress of the case, Palmer was glad of the opportunity of saying, "I don't believe that's something that should be discussed at the funeral." It sounded so much better than saying, "I don't have the slightest idea what to do next."

SINCE HE WAS ALL DRESSED UP in his uniform, Knutson thought that he could at least show himself around the Court House. Orly Peterson had entered Knutson's office and was sitting on the chair in front of the sheriff's desk waiting for him.

"So, how was the funeral?"

"It was sad. What did you expect? I think Stover's mother held up as well as possible, and my brother did his usual 'the world has been diminished' thing."

"Big crowd?"

"Yah, the church was pretty full. A lot of college kids were there. All in all, though, I don't like funerals. They remind me of my own mortality. I especially don't like ones for murder victims. In many of the Agatha Christie books, the murderer can't resist seeing his victim eugologized. I gotta say, I didn't see any likely killers."

"You know, that's what I wanted to talk to you about. With your permission, I'd like to pursue the political line of investigation."

Knutson blinked. "The political line? What do you mean?"

"Well, it's like this. There's clearly no known motive for the murder of Stover Stordahl. The way I got it figured, it's got to be for money—a lot of money, I'd say. So, if we're looking for a motive that involves a lot of money, where do we look? What's the biggest deal going down? The ethanol plant, that's what. Somebody is going to make a lot of money on that. So, I figure, Stover's a bird watcher, right? So say he goes out someplace to watch birds and he sees somebody evaluating a site for the ethanol plant. So maybe this is top secret, and if the word gets out it'll cost somebody a lot of money or, get this, a lot of votes. That takes us back to the congressman and that sleezy administrative aide of his. I checked to see if Representative Paulson was in Washington this weekend. He was not! Now, we don't know if he was in Fergus Falls, but we don't know he wasn't either. Even if he wasn't, that little toady of his could act on his own. Eliminate Stover as a possible monkey wrench in the gears and the project goes forward. That's a pretty good motive, I'd say."

"Maybe, but aren't you forgetting something? The medical examiner said that he was probably attacked late Saturday night or early Sunday morning. Stover would hardly be out watching birds at night. As you have perhaps noticed, it is dark out then."

"So what. The M.E. might be one hundred percent right about that forensic evidence, but that does not mean that the victim could not have been incapacitated for a time and then done away with. Suppose this administrative assistant finds Stover where he shouldn't be. Suppose he conks him on the head or maybe ties him up and then calls Paulson and asks him what he should do. Suppose Paulson tells him to wait until dark and then handle the problem. What do you think?"

The sheriff was nodding his head as Orly presented his theory. "Not bad. It holds together. And it's not as though we have an overwhelming number of leads to follow. Yah, go ahead and look into it. But do it discretely. You don't want to mess with something that could backfire with a lot of bad publicity for either the congressman or for us, nor do you want to put anyone on their guard. Yah, go ahead, nose around and see what you can find out."

As Orly got up to leave, the front desk called. "There are two, er, gentlemen to see you, Sheriff. Shall I send them in?"

Palmer could think of no good reason not to delay doing nothing, so he said, "Yup."

TWO MEN ENTERED HIS OFFICE, bringing with them the unmistakable smell of beer and cigarette smoke. It did not take enormous powers of deduction to determine their previous habitat. Chief Foss and another man ambled into his office and plopped themselves down on the two chairs in front of his desk. He had been rather avoiding Chief for the last twenty years, ever since he had quit the town softball team. In truth, Palmer just stopped enjoying the game, especially since Chief always put so much emphasis on winning. Palmer was an average outfielder with an average arm and carried a less than an eye-popping batting average. Chief had a way of making everyone feel that with every out they made they had let the team, to say nothing of the whole city, down. When he had quit, he politely said that he felt that he had grown too old and that it was time for a younger man to take his place. This had only led Chief to make continued references to his age. Whenever he would see the sheriff, he would say, "How yah doin', Old Man?" It had gotten more tiresome with each passing year. The other man he did not know.

A slave to tedious consistency, Chief said: "How yah doin' Old Man? Do you know "Shots" here?"

The sheriff knitted his brows in fake concentration and said, "No, I don't think I've had the pleasure."

"I'm John Christiansen," Shots said, carefully accenting the first name.

"Nice to meet you. Now, what can I do for you boys?" When he said it, Palmer wondered, *Why did I just call 'em boys? Whatever, it seems to fit.*

"It's this deal with Homer Grimstead," Chief began.

"But Homer died last week," Palmer interjected.

"Yah, that's the whole problem. He stood up in our meeting last month and said that he was going to leave us eighty acres of land just south of town that we could use as a hunting preserve. Well, I looked into that, and I discovered that before we could take possession of that, we had to be incorporated, as they say. So I got together with that old shiny pants lawyer, Eldon Steele—Hey, what did the lawyer name his daughter?"

"Huh?"

"What did the lawyer name his daughter?"

"I donno."

` "Sue. Get it? Sue. So anyway, I went to the lawyer and he said it was a simple thing and so he helped me fill out the forms and get the signatures and I paid some money—I'd better get some of that back from you guys, Shots—and I thought that was that. So, I told this to Homer and he said that he had taken care of everything and put it in his will. But then what happens? Homer kicks off a lot sooner than we thought. You know, the way he was still putting down the beer last month, he seemed to be as good as ever, but I guess even then the cancer was out to get him.

"So what happens? We find out now that there is no such will. That the only will is some old thing that Homer signed years ago leaving everything to his nephew, that ne'er-do-well wuss who wouldn't know a shotgun from a fishing pole. I ran into him yesterday and asked him about our land. He said he didn't know anything about a new will. So I asked him, 'Didn't your uncle ever tell you that he was going to give us that land south of town to our club?' and he said that he knew that his uncle was quite the sportsman and that he may have considered something like that, but that he and his uncle didn't really talk all that much and that as far as he knew that land would now belong to him.

"I didn't know whether to believe him or not. At first I thought he was shittin' me, but then he said that he really didn't know all about wills and such and that such things would be handled by the courts and that maybe there was another will after all and gave me a nasty little grin and scooted off. If I'd had my gun, I think I would have shot that Goddamn little". . .(there followed a stream of profainty so vile, yet so creative that it left Palmer breathless, but filled with reluctant admiration as well).

Palmer stood and held his hand up in the universal stop signal. "Hold it right there, Chief. I was in the army, and I know all the cuss words. I'm no prude. But I don't want to hear that kind of language in the office of the Sheriff of Otter Tail County. I'm elected to serve the people, and the people will not want their servant to be talked to like that. Besides, what would happen if you said something that later would have legal consequences? I don't want to stand up in court and say that Chief Foss called Jack Grimstead a "Goddamn little. . . er, what you just said."

"All right, all right, sorry about that, but it made me so goddamn—sorry—mad."

"Were you there, too, er, John? What do you know about this?"

Christiansen said, "I was the guy that was pushing our club into doing more in the line of conservation and preservation. I've been looking up things and trying to find out the best way of putting into writing what the club should be. In fact, I've been writing our new constitution, just like Thomas Jefferson."

"Actually," Knutson put in, "Jefferson didn't write the constitution. He was in France at the time."

Christiansen looked at him with a mixture of admiration and annoyance. "That so? Well, anyhoo, I got to thinking that we should name the land that we were supposed to get from Homer after him, you know, the "Homer Grimstead Hunting Preserve" or something like that. If fact, someone even suggested we change the name of the whole club to something like the "Grimstead Sportsmen's Association." Well, I thought that was dumb idea, but I thought maybe I'd run the idea past Homer to see what he thought about it. So I did. I called him up. He sounded very touched and grateful, although, now that I think about it, this may have been either because he was in pain from the cancer or he had put away a few too many jars of beer. But, anyhoo, the point is that when I talked to him about it, he told me that it was all taken care of. See what we're getting at?"

"Suppose you tell me," Palmer said dryly.

"It's just this," Chief cut in. "We think that Jack Grimstead has done something with the will and that he will sell the land and get whatever he can for it. I mean, how much can that be? It isn't worth much. Would it hurt him to go through with his uncle's wishes even if they can't find a new will? Now I know that old Homer wasn't the sharpest tool in the shed, especially the last year or so, but I think we all believed him about that. He knew what he wanted to do. If he hadn't been full of cancer, I would suspect the son of a , uh , guy of murdering his uncle. So, what I'm saying is, we don't want to let Jack get away with it."

"What do you think I can do about it," Palmer asked.

"How should we know? We ain't lawyers."

"It may be, you know, that might be the best thing to do. Consult Eldon Steele again, or somebody else if you didn't like him. We don't make the laws, we just enforce them."

"Can't you at least investigate to see if the law has been broken?"

Palmer inwardly groaned. Nothing good could come from this. Still, it was an election year, and, should he really decide to run again, the last thing he wanted to do was to offend sportsmen. He remembered four years ago when the National Rifle Association discovered that his wife had been openly demonstrating against them and writing letters to the newspaper denouncing Congressman Paulson as being one of their fully paid agents. It had gotten nasty. "Is any of this official? Has the probate court even looked at the will yet? Do you know the first thing about it? These things take time, you know. I'll tell you what. I'll nose around and ask a few questions. But don't get out in front of this whole thing. If there's only one will and Homer left everything to his nephew, well, that's just the way it is. Perfectly legal. In fact, I'd advise you to be nice to him and maybe he'll still let you hunt on his land."

"Our land."

"Whatever."

The sheriff ushered them out and as he did so he caught sight of a vaguely familiar reporter from the

Fargo Forum. He quickly closed the door. That was all he needed! A chat with a reporter followed by the next day's headline reading "Otter Tail Sheriff has no idea of what he is doing!" He couldn't hide in his office forever, he realized, so he had to do something that would make him look like a man of action. What to do? The beery odor that still hung in the office gave him an inspiration. He'd follow up on Chief's request to talk to Jack Grimstead!

P ALMER COULD NOT RECALL EVER MEETING THE MAN, so he looked in the telephone book to see where Grimstead had his office. Ah, Grimstead Progressive Real Estate—Kaddatz Building—Fergus Falls—right on his way home! He grabbed his jacket and purposefully strode out of his office. The reporter stood and said, "Sheriff, if you could just spare a few minutes . . ." to which Knutson replied, "Sorry, 'fraid not. Maybe tomorrow," and was gone.

The Kaddatz Hotel had seen better days, then worse days, and was now in the process of seeing better days again. For years it had stood forlornly empty, a sad reminder of the glory days before the interstate had caused all the hotels to move to the outskirts of town. It had not been restored to its former glory, perhaps, but it was now refurbished to the point where it was once again one of the more impressive downtown buildings. Palmer read the directory inside the entryway and found Grimstead Progressive Real Estate. The thought occurred to him, "Why Progressive? Has there ever been an unprogressive real estate business?"

The sheriff opened the door and saw a tall man with a weak chin and square glasses look up at him with what appeared to be a look of terror. He had thinning red hair and looked to be in his late thirties. "Oh," he said, "you startled me. I wasn't expecting anyone."

Knutson looked at the sparse furnishings and the layer of dust on the file cabinet and thought, *Obviously you haven't expected anyone for weeks*, but said, "I'm Sheriff Palmer Knutson. Could I have a word with you?"

"Sheriff? Um, um, I haven't done anything."

"I didn't say you had. May I sit down?"

"Of course, of course. How may I help you. I have just learned of the proposed sale of about a quarter of land on Lake Henjum that could be turned into some very nice lots. Not the best swimming beach, I suppose, but a lovely site, and with a good road. I could probably get you a real good deal at this early time of the year."

Palmer unzipped his jacket and looked hopefully for a coffee pot. There was none. "No, I'm not shopping for land today, I just wanted to ask you a couple of questions. First of all, I understand that your uncle died last week. I knew him a little bit. Um, my sympathies."

"Thank you. That's very kind."

"Well, that's a little bit about why I wanted to talk to you. I heard from a couple of guys that he had planned to leave some land for some kind of hunting preserve. They claim that he had set it up in his will and that now you are telling people that you own it. They are kind of upset and are making all sorts of wild claims that you altered his will and are now claiming it for yourself. I thought I'd better have a talk with you before the whole thing gets out of hand."

Grimstead let out a long and exaggerated sigh and said, "Oh Lord, I can just guess who that might be. First of all, I don't know about my uncle's will. As far as I know, he kept it in his safety deposit box in the bank and that hasn't been opened yet. As a matter of fact, he did talk to me about that issue about a month ago. He said he was thinking about it but he wasn't sure how to do it. He went to see old man Monson in the bank, but as I understand it, there were all sorts of legal things that they had to do first. That hunting club that Chief Foss is in wasn't even incorporated. He's going around town saying that I'm stealing their land. I really don't know anything about it. Last time he talked to me about his will, Uncle Homer implied that I was the heir to all his fortune, including that hideous old Cadillac. I do know that he had a legal will made up several years ago. In fact, he reminded me of that just last month. I really don't know anything about how all that stuff works, so the day after my uncle died, I went over to see my lawyer, the guy who handles my real estate things, Julius Ahoel, of Ahoel, Ahoel, and Nelson. He talked to a judge and we got a court order to open up the safety deposit box tomorrow, so maybe we will find out then. Maybe he did get the whole thing together and leave that worthless land to the hunters, I don't know, but I've certainly had nothing to do with it. Frankly, I'd appreciate it if, next time you see him, you'd tell Chief to shut up about something he knows nothing about. That kind of talk isn't going to do my business any good."

The sheriff realized that he hadn't heard a single specific in the ravings of Chief and Shots and said, "Yeah, well, maybe things will cool off. Speaking of business, I understand that you purchased Nora's Knitting Nook. How that going?"

"Oh, that. I closed the doors yesterday. I just kept it open to liquidate the inventory, which wasn't much. I just bought the property as an investment."

"An investment?"

"Yeah, well, I might as well tell you. It'll be made public pretty soon anyhow. I heard that Monson, the guy who ran First Federal of Fergus Falls—he died, last week, did you know that?"

"Yeah, I did. Heart attack, I guess."

"So they say. Well, anyway, I heard that he had bought up property on both sides of Nora's Knitting Nook. I thought there might be something going on, so I went over there and talked to Nora. She didn't really want to talk business, but then I got her to go on and on about Norwegian yarn and how they set up those sweater patterns and the next thing you know I've got her talking about her business and she lets on that she is thinking of selling out and that someone had made her an offer on her property. So before too long she tells me that it was Monson who wanted it and she even let it slip what he'd offered her. I'm thinking he wants this property pretty badly. So I went back to my office and scraped together all the assets I figured I could lay my hands on and came back and said that not only would I offer her two thousand dollars more than Monson offered her, but that I would take over her inventory. I presume she thought that I was saying that I was going to continue the business, and I said nothing to let her think otherwise. So, anyway, in a couple of days I bought the property. In a couple of weeks I'd gotten rid of a lot of old yarn and knitting needles. Two days before he died, old Monson came over to make me an offer.

"Well, I used to work in the bank, and me and Monson didn't exactly see eye to eye, if you know what I mean, 'So I understand you own this place now,' he says. And I say, 'Sure do. Wanna buy some yarn?' And he sneers at me and says, 'I know damn well why you bought this place, and it has nothing to do with running a small business. How much do you want?' So I told him. Frankly, I thought he was going to have a heart attack right there and then. Clearly, the way he was buying the other property on the block meant that he wanted to add to the size of his bank, and I figured that Nora's Knitting Nook, being right in the middle of the block, made it pretty valuable. But hey, I didn't want to scuttle the deal, the last thing I wanted was to be left with that white elephant. So he calms down and I come down and he comes up, and we piss and moan and finally split the difference. Now, I can't say he was real happy with the deal, but we shook hands and he gave me a week to vacate the premises."

Palmer was, in spite of himself, rather intrigued by the machinations of business, and asked, "And his death, that has done nothing to squelch the deal?"

Jack Grimstead looked extremely pleased with himself. "Nope. We did the whole deal the next day. So now I suppose the bank, or maybe his widow, owns it. I don't, and I got the money in the bank. As a matter of fact, it was that extra cash that enabled me to buy that lake property I just offered you."

Palmer leaned forward, "To tell you the truth, I heard that you had made some fine deal, but I didn't know what it was."

"Really?" said Grimstead, with a note of cautious surprise. "Who told you that?"

"As you know—well, as everybody knows—I've been investigating the murder of Stover Stordahl. He had been part of that Otter Tail County Bird Watching and Conservation Society, so I went and talked to Carolyn Dahl, who's the president. I also spoke with her daughter, since she'd seen him earlier that day. It seems that you went out with her on the night he was killed. I just asked if she had been downtown and if she'd noticed anything out of the ordinary, or if she had seen Stover walking around. I didn't pry into your affairs, but she said that you spoke about making a good real estate deal, that's all."

"You know, that was one of the longest evenings in my life. I'm surprised she'd mention that I said that, because it was one of the few sentences that I had the opportunity to speak all night. In fact, I was all set to explain it to her when she interrupted to tell me some inane fact about her college career. Looking back on it, I don't know why I asked her out in the first place. I suppose it was because I hadn't been able to afford to take a woman out for supper in a long time. I don't think there will be a second date."

In spite of his distasteful business opportunism, Palmer was beginning to like the man. "So," he said, as he began to position his feet to stand, "she said you brought her home about 10:30, is that right?"

"Yeah, why do you ask."

"Did you go right home?"

"Yeah, I suppose I did. Why"

"It's just that we have reason to believe that Stordahl was murdered around midnight. That would mean that you probably were not around downtown at the time, that's all."

Grimstead visibly paled, "Horrible, horrible," he muttered. "No, I'm afraid that at that time I was in bed. Alone, as usual."

Palmer stood with one hand on the doorknob. "Meanwhile, if I see Chief Foss, I'll just tell him to hold his horses until the legal stuff is settled. But fair warning. If you end up with that land and they lose their dream of a hunting paradise, you won't be a popular man."

"I think I can handle it. I've never been too popular in my life."

Chapter Sixteen

CHIEF DEPUTY ORLY PETERSON walked into the small District Office of Congressman Glenn Paulson on the ground floor of the Kaddatz Building. The decor consisted of large framed pictures of the congressman and several American flags. Behind the desk, Chadd Hangar gave him an unwelcome glance and grunted, "What can I do for you?"

Peterson put on a friendly face and said, "My name is Orly Peterson. I'm the Chief Deputy of Otter Tail County. I just wondered if I may have a few words with you?"

"What about?"

Not expecting anything quite so direct, Orly hemmed and hawed and finally came up with: "I just thought that with all the developments that'll happen with the new ethanol facility, we should, you know, just touch bases. I mean, this'll bring in a lot of business, a lot of new workers. There'll be construction issues, you know, such as if we have to close off a highway during construction, that sort of thing. I've always felt that it is better to be proactive on a big project like this, and I thought that the more we knew about it, well, the better prepared we would be to handle things as they arise."

"Ummph, I guess so. What do you want to know?"

Orly paused to study his possible suspect. He was dressed once again in a three-piece suit adorned with a flag pin and set off with a red white and blue tie. This had essentially been his uniform in college, where Hangar had majored in political science, was president of the Young Republicans Club and the College Citizens for Life, and had attempted to found a national organization of College Students Against Liberal Professors. He had graduated before the organization could be organized, however, and rued the fact that he could not find another to take up the banner. The Benedictine brothers at his all male college were slightly afraid of him and often referred to him as Torquemada. Had he known this, he would have seen it as a compliment, although he considered that if he had been in charge of the Spanish Inquisition, he would not have been such a sissy. There was no right wing agenda too extreme for him, and he longed to serve the people in a way that would show them the light. He searched for a champion, and found one in Glenn Paulson. After interviewing for the job of administrative assistant, Paulson found him to be just what he had been looking for. As one of Hangar's college classmates, an afficianado of *The Simpsons*, remarked, he would now have the opportunity to play Smithers to Paulson's Mr. Burns. In his universe, sycophancy had its own rewards. He was a mole-like creature, prematurely balding at age twenty-four, with beady eyes that perpetually darted right and left and never focused on the person to whom he was talking. Orly Peterson felt an instant revulsion.

"So, how's this all supposed to work," Peterson asked.

Here was an opportunity for Hangar to show off. "All right, you get the corn, locally produced, mind you, and you can store it on the site. Then the corn is run through hammer mills that grind it into a fine powder that they call meal. They mix the meal with water and alpha-amylase, an enzyme—know what an enzyme is?—well anyway, this begins the conversion from starch to sugar. What you have then is the mash, and you have to cook this at a high temperature to sterilize it, then you cool it in a cooling vessel. At that point you add yeast and pump it into individual tanks for fermentation—that converts the sugar into ethanol. Heat and carbon dioxide are byproducts of this, so you have to eliminate heat through a series of heat exchanges and you can collect the carbon dioxide and compress it for industrial purposes. After about sixty hours of fermentation, the 'beer,' as they call it, is transferred into a final tank, at which point it contains about fifteen percent ethanol.

"Now then, this 'beer'—I wouldn't drink it if I were you—is pumped into a continuous flow distillation unit. Since the alcohol evaporates at a lower temperature than water, it'll leave the top of the final column at about ninety-six percent strength. The remaining water is removed by molecular sieves and five percent gasoline is added to the ethanol to denature it and make it ready for shipping. It's really quite simple, really."

Peterson, in spite of himself, was impressed by the young man's knowledge, but regarded the imparter of the knowledge with the warmth he felt for tele-marketers. "And so, that's distributed and winds up in our tanks, right?"

"Yes, eventually, but there is more to it. There are the bi-products. I've already mentioned carbon dioxide. Besides this, the remaining mash, called 'stillage' at this point, is transferred to a centerfuge where the components can be separated. Wet stillage and distillers grains are high in protein and can be recombined as feed for livestock. Everybody wins."

"So, this must really be a high priority for you?"

"Well, not for me personally, you understand. I just serve the Congressman. But for him, it certainly is. He'll be the chair of the House Agriculture Committee one day and, depending on the administration, he could very well become the Secretary of Agriculture. A successful ethanol operation in his own district could become a national showcase of how we can be engergy independent through farming."

"And how are things going?" Peterson asked.

"Fantastic. We expect to announce the site of the ethanol plant within the next few days. We believe we have found an ideal site that will pass all environmental tests and will be in an ideal place for transportation."

"Ah," Orly said coyly, "were there any difficulties in attaining this site?"

"What do you mean?" Hangar asked sharply, his piggy eyes darting everywhere but toward the deputy's face.

"I just thought that wherever this will be built, it'll be somewhat of a windfall for the property owner. You must have had to do some pretty cagey spadework."

Sweat began to from along Hangar's elevated hairline. "No, no, nothing difficult at all. We were very fortunate the way it all developed."

"Well, good for you, and good for the congressman." Orly began to rise and in his best Colombo immitation said, "Oh, there's just one more thing. As you know there was a murder in our community last weekend. We're asking everybody if they saw or heard anything that could be of help to us. The victim, um, Stover Stordahl was his name, was quite the bird watcher, it seems, and he might have been out in the country Saturday afternoon. I mean, if you were investigating sites for the plant, well, maybe you might have seen him. Were you out in the country last Saturday?"

The sweat on Hangar's forehead grew in volume. "Yes, I heard all about that. Terrible, terrible. As it turns out, I was out investigating our site on Saturday, but I certainly didn't see him."

"So, you knew him? You knew what he looked like?"

"No, no, of course not. I just meant that I didn't see anybody."

"What about that night. Were you out last Saturday night?"

Peterson had not noticed the slight nervous tic on the side of Hangar's face before. He did now as the aide said, "No. I was home all night. Alone.

"Now that's not really true, is it. I understand that you were at the Blue Fox at around midnight."

"What? Who told you that. No, never mind, I can guess. It was that dreadful woman with the space between her teeth. In any event, it was so unimportant I just forgot about it, that's all."

"Didn't get lucky, Huh?"

"What do you mean by that? And . . . wait a minute. Why are you asking me this?"

"Oh, I just thought if you'd been around town you might have seen the victim, that's all. He liked to go for evening walks."

"Ah, yes, I see. No, I'm afraid that I can't help you."

"That's too bad. Oh, well, thank's for all the info on the ethanol plant. We'll keep in touch."

LATER THAT EVENING, ORLY WENT to the apartment of his fiance, Allysha Holm, to share a pizza. She was a recent graduate of Minnesota State University, Moorhead, and was in her first year of directing the special education program of the Fergus Falls school district. With her deep blue eyes, thin nose, and full lips, she appeared to have stepped off a "Visit Sweden" poster. She really was a breathtakingly beautiful young woman, a fact of which Orly was all too aware. She wore an oversized MSUM sweatshirt and, as Orly had slyly determined as he gave her a passionate hug at the door, nothing under it. He had been droping hints that perhaps they should move in together, but Allysha steadfastly refused. She was in the process of planning the wedding in her home town of Moorhead, and every time they had gotten together for the last few months Orly had been duty-bound to listen and pretend to be interested in such things as flowers, ring bearers, musical numbers, invitations, photographers, reception plans and guest lists. That he was consistently able to fake enthusiasm was a testament to his love.

They were seated on the sofa, behind a coffee table on which reposed the latest three issues of *Modern Bride*. Orly had consumed his half of the pizza and was wondering if he would be offered more of her half or whether he should just act natural and unaware and take another piece. Allysha said, "So, how are you coming along on your murder investigation? Any leads?"

Orly was perfectly willing to tell her everything he knew, but he thought it necessary to project the ethical professionalism that the situation seemed to call for. "You know, I can't really talk too much about it at this point," leaving out the "because there is nothing much to say"—"Sheriff Knutson is following his own leads, I think, although I'm not one hundred percent sure of what they are. But I had an idea that I ran by him this afternoon, and he seemed to find it interesting. He told me to run with it."

"Ooh, what is it. I won't tell anybody."

"Oh, I know you won't. It's just that, well, all right, I'll tell you. I think there could be a political element here. As I was telling Knutson, murder is most often done for money. Follow the money and you can't go wrong. And where's all the money these days? I'll tell you. Ethanol. Congressman Paulson and his aide have a lot of political capital invested in this whole thing, because it's going to make a lot of people rich. Knutson once said that if we could find out where Stordahl was murdered, we might be able to know both why and who. I figure the most likely place would be somewhere that has something to do with that ethanol plant.

"So, anyway, I went right over to Paulson's regional office today and questioned the aide. I think he acted suspicious."

Allysha's beautiful eyes widened. "He did? How?"

If there can be swagger in a voice, Orly had it. "I just asked him if he could account for his whereabouts on Saturday afternoon and night, at the time when Stover was murdered."

"Well, could he?"

"Not at all. In fact, I caught him out in a lie. I gotta admit, I didn't like him much. He looks like a rodent and he seems overly, I don't know, greasy. Like if he would have freckles they would just slide off. Whether or not he could really be a murderer, well, I just don't know. Like I said, I didn't like him. He gave me the creeps."

"I suppose that means that you won't be asking him to be your best man, then. But speaking of that . . ."

Chapter Seventeen

THE TELEPHONE RANG AT 6:45. Palmer fumbled for the bedside phone, dropped it on the floor, accidentally knocked it under the bed, got up, went to his knees, and fished around blindly until he found it. "Yah, hello"

"Is this Sheriff Palmer Knutson?"

"Yah. What's happened?"

"That's what I'm calling about. My name is Dan Davebom. I'm a reporter for the *Minneapolis StarTribune*."

"Yah, so, what do you want?"

"A story has just come out on wire service that you have a prime suspect in the Stordahl murder and that an arrest is imminent. I was wondering if a press conference will soon be called and what you can tell me in the meantime."

"I have no idea what you are talking about," the sheriff said, now fully awake.

"According to a reporter for the *Fergus Falls Daily Journal*, one Stacie Ryan, you implied that you knew the identify of the murderer and were just waiting to complete the gathering of evidence."

"I did not," Palmer said indignantly. "What am I supposed to have said?"

"According to this reporter, you were quoted as saying, 'I have a real good idea who is behind this, but I'm keeping it to myself?' Do you deny saying that?"

With a sickening feeling, Knutson realized that it did sound awfully familiar. He said, "Yah, well, I may have said something like that, but I didn't mean it."

"You didn't mean it? Can I quote you on that?"

Palmer saw headlines that read, "Sheriff lies to reporter!" and said, "No, please, you don't understand. That whole conversation has to be taken in context. I attempted to imply that we were developing a profile of the murderer. When I said I had 'a real good idea of who,' what I meant was, a real good idea of the type of person who would commit this crime. I do not have a specific person in mind." When he said it, Palmer inwardly congratulated himself, *Hey, that was not too bad for quick thinking. I wonder if he will buy it.*

"Is that on the record?"

Knutson realized that it was the best he was likely to come up with, so he said, "Yah, I suppose so. Just indicate that we are making progress." This was, of course, as much of a lie as the original quote, but something could always drop from the sky.

"Well, thanks. I hope I didn't get you up." (Palmer was tempted to explain that it was perfectly fine since he had to get up to crawl under the bed and answer the phone anyway, but thought such levity might be inappropriate.) "Is there anything else you would like to add at this time."

"Nope. When I do, you'll find out about it."

"All right, thanks, Sheriff."

Palmer hung up the telephone and flopped back down on the bed and dreaded going to work.

"Who was that, dear?" Ellie asked.

"Some reporter from the *Strib*. You know what, Ellie? Your husband has a bi-i-i-i-g mouth!"

* *

As Palmer walked into the Court House he spotted Orly striding forward to meet him. "So. You know who it is? Why didn't your tell me? The phone's been ringing steadily ever since the paper came out. What gives?"

"Come into my office," was all the sheriff said. He stopped to get a cup of coffee, took one gulp, fought off a gag reflex, and remained wordless until he had closed the door behind them. "No, I do not know who did it. No, I do not have a suspect. No, I don't have a real plan of what to do next, and, yes, if I ever shoot my mouth off like that again I should be shot. That reporter, Stacie Ryan, one of Ellie's friends, got me at a weak moment. I didn't want to appear to be helpless, and I thought I should reassure people a little bit. Clearly, I overstated the situation. Overstated! *Fa'en in Helveta!* (a rather strong Norwegian curse) I lied like a rug! But I didn't mean to. Look, I don't want to handle all this now. I'll get that reporter on the phone and try to get her to print some kind of clarification. Meanwhile, here's the line. Tell everybody who asks that I meant that we had some sort of composite murderer in mind with no specific name, or some nonsense like that."

"Sure, okay, I can do that. But you really don't have any suspect in mind?"

Palmer sighed, "I think I have made myself abundantly clear on that. And tell the receptionist that I will not take any more calls from reporters today."

The sheriff sat and pondered what to do next. He had to face up to calling Stacie Ryan. She had quoted him exactly, and it wasn't fair to her to imply misunderstanding when she had merely imputed real meaning into a straightforward comment. Besides, she was Ellie's friend. Reluctantly, he called her at her office at the *Daily Journal*. She was exceedingly chipper.

"Hi, Palmer. Did you see the article? The whole state is talking about it."

"Um, well, that's something I need to talk to you about." Grimly he told her the entire truth, as well as his face saving version that he used on Dan Davebom. He explained his motivation for exaggerating his progress, and hoped that she would be able to write a follow-up article that would introduce the right amount of obfuscation. He was pleased to discover that, although she was disappointed that she was not on the cusp of a genuine scoop, she would do what she could, even if it meant backtracking on her story. Palmer concluded his call with "And Stacie, when I do find out who did this—and I will— I will personally call you first."

The conversation made him feel a little bit better, and he was able to concentrate on his crossword puzzle. There was still that nagging bit about that hunting club, and the obvious dissatisfaction of everyone concerned, that was swirling around about old Homer Grimstead's land. Jack Grimstead had indicated that they were going to open the safety deposit box that morning. Perhaps if he had a little talk with someone at the bank . . . He didn't even know who was in charge over there since old man Munson had shuffled off his mortal coil. At least he could find that out.

When he called the bank, they informed him that Alice Monson, the wife of the late Aldwin Monson, was now the president of the bank and that all inquiries were to be handled by her. Through her secretary, Palmer arranged for a meeting at one o'clock. He thought about proceeding with the filing of papers for reelection. Then he didn't.

CONSIDERING THAT THE WHOLE TOWN had perhaps read the *Daily Journal* and had digested contents of the Stacie Ryan story, Palmer realized that the last thing he wanted to do that day was to appear in a public place to eat his lunch. Therefore, before coming to work he had created a magnificent sandwich of roast beef, mayonnaise, crisp lettuce, and a little hint of horseradish. Hunkered down in his office, he did not enjoy it as much as he had intended, for instead of savoring every bite, as he usually did, he stared at the wall, trying to think of the next step in the Stordahl murder case. Finally, he got up and went into Orly's office.

"Hey, Orly, I'm going on over to the First Federal Bank about one o'clock. Want to come along?"

The deputy furled his brow and said, "Yeah, I suppose. Why? What do they have to do with Stover Stordahl?"

The sheriff shrugged and said, "Nothing, as far as I know. But have you heard all that stuff about Homer Grimstead supposedly giving some land to that hunting club? I had a couple guys in my office yesterday and they as much as accused Homer's nephew of stealing it from them. Homer did all his business with Aldwin Monson, who, as you know, conveniently died the day after Homer. They're all worked up about it and I said I'd look into it, so I'm going over to the bank to talk to Aldwin's widow. It just might be better if we were on the same page with that."

"Yeah, okay, sure. Hey, did you hear about when Ole went on a Caribbean Cruise? It's funnier than a rubber crutch."

Palmer interrupted, "That's a terrible expression! In a public office like this, we have to show some political correctness, but, you know, that's really tasteless. Making fun of the handicapped! Where did you hear such a thing?"

"Er, actually, I heard it from you. I thought it was pretty funny."

Knutson audibly sighed and leaned against the door frame. "Oh, well, all right, then, go ahead."

Orly was already chuckling, and began, "So this cruise went to the Bahamas, see, and Ole goes into a night club in Nassau. And there's this black six-foot-six master of ceremonies who goes from table to table. He says to Ole, 'If you can guess my riddle, you may have a drink on the house.' Well Ole says that sounds like a pretty good deal so he's willing to try, and the guy says, 'My mother's only sister had only one nephew and my father's only brother had only one nephew—Nieces were there none. Now can you tell me who was the only son?' Well, Ole thought for a while and said, 'Yew got me dere, I don't tink I can tell yew.' And the big m.c. roars and says, 'It is me!!'"

"So Ole, he laughs along with everyone else and thinks it's pretty good. He gets back to Minnesota and meets Swen and says, 'Sven, I got a riddle for you. Now listen carefully. I am not my uncle's only niece, and my nephew is an only son. Who am I?' Well, as you might expect, Swen is bewildered and says, 'I can't figger dat out. Who are yew?' And Ole says, "I'm this great big colored guy in Nassau.'"

Desperately seeking something to cheer himself up, Palmer actually laughed. He was somewhat ashamed of himself for doing so, but Orly was delighted. As a postscript, he said, "Oh, that Ole. Let's go to the bank."

The sheriff could not remember the last time he had ever been in the First Federal of Fergus Falls. He used to do his banking at the Fergus Falls branch of a national mega-bank, but one day when he had a simple question on his account, he had tried to call up and ask the most minor of questions. He faced six separate menus on the telephone before he finally reached a human voice. He did not have patience for this, and was already outraged by the time an actual person spoke to him. "Are you a real person?" he had asked. Upon being assured in a patronizing voice that she was, Palmer nevertheless asked, "Are you sure?" Reassurance came with a rather snotty tone and so Palmer tried to lighten things up by making a comment on the weather. The voice on the other end of the conversation said she wouldn't know. When asked to explain, she told Palmer that she was in Sioux Falls, South Dakota. Palmer said, "I'm calling about my account in a bank two blocks away and I have to talk to someone in South Dakota?" The customer relations expert explained the situation and asked how she could help. Palmer said she couldn't and later that day moved all his money into the smallest local bank in town. The action made him feel rather good.

First Federal was considerably larger than his bank, and had grown spectacularly over the last fifteen years. Palmer was impressed with the subtle pastels that made up the carpet and the fine desks with new flat screen computer monitors. Clearly, Alvin Monson must have known his onions. When Palmer and Orly presented themselves to the receptionist at 12:58, she telephoned Alice Monson to announce their arrival. She had them wait a full ninety seconds and showed them in.

The sheriff had never met Mrs. Monson. He expected a woman who would be the counterpart of the elderly banker, perhaps a blue-haired lady in an expensive but frumpy house dress. As he entered the office he saw a fifty-year-old woman in a short black jacket and a mid-thigh length Scottish kilt held together by what Palmer would have described as a giant safety pin. She looked very smart. He looked past her in search of the widow. The woman advanced and held out her arm and said, "I'm Alice Monson. You must be Sheriff Knutson. How may I help you?"

The hand that Palmer shook wore a ring with a diamond as big as a walnut. An elegant string of pearls hung loosely around her neck. He stammered, "Yes, I'm Palmer Knutson, and this here is Orly Peterson, my Chief Deputy."

"Please sit down," she said, as she resumed her place behind a massive desk that held little more than a telephone.

Accepting the invitation, Palmer began, "I just wanted to clear up something that seems to have a lot of people upset. It's about that land that Homer Grimstead was supposed to give to the Fergus Falls Fin and Feather Club."

Alice Monson rolled her eyes and said, "Oh, God, I should have known. I've about had my fill of that nonsense. Look, Aldwin was a good man, and he was a pretty good small town banker, if it came to that. But he never could get away from small town attitudes. You may or may not know it, but I'm his second wife. His first wife died about twenty years ago and was, apparently, a saint, at least that was the impression that

Aldwin imparted to me. We met at a Minnesota Bankers convention about four years later. He was a lonely man and I had just, well, we don't need to get into that. Anyway, I had my MBA and when he brought me back to Fergus Falls, I saw all sorts of promise for this bank. It has really been a time of marvelous and steady growth for us ever since."

"So," Palmer said as he began to take in the fine artwork on the walls of the office, "you've had a part in the running of the bank for some time?"

"Yes. Aldwin remained as president, of course, but my role in the institution has been increasing all along. Aldwin remained the face of the bank, and he met with the old customers. That really was what he was best at. But that, unfortunately, is what has gotten us into somewhat of a bind."

"Er, how do you mean?' asked Knutson.

"For instance, I remember the day when I saw Aldwin meeting with some old codger and some younger guy I vaguely recognized. It caught my attention because the old guy was probably deaf and kept shouting, and the younger guy sat there like a urine sample. After they left, I asked Aldwin what that was all about, and he said that it was an old customer who had been banking with us since God was a boy and that he wanted to change his will. I told him that that was nothing that should concern us, that we didn't want to get into that business, but he said that he had witnessed the old man's will before because he didn't want to deal with lawyers. He said it was all legal, and I suppose it was. I mean, this was just something that Aldwin always did, so I let it pass."

"So was there a new will? Did Aldwin witness a new document?"

"That's where it gets hazy. To tell you the truth, perhaps I didn't listen closely enough to him. I was in the process of putting together that big deal with the ethanol refinery, and we had just announced it that day. I had spent several hours with that sleazy congressman who has been in the pocket of the coal-and-oil men for years and who now almost claims to have invented the concept of alternative fuel."

Palmer, mindful of how Ellie would have enjoyed the description, mumbled a, "Yeah, I know what you mean."

"Yes, he's horrible, isn't he? Anyway, we had a big ceremony at the university to announce it. I suppose I wasn't in the mood to hear about an old man and a bunch of hunters. One hundred million dollars is a big deal for any bank! In any event, I do remember Aldwin saying that he told the old guy that he would have to do something more about making sure that the club was incorporated and that it would have to be a legal entity. I saw the old coot and the younger man go down to the safety deposit room after meeting with Aldwin and there was some speculation that Homer Grimstead had put a document in the safety deposit box that would indicate his intentions. In the event, it appears that he did not."

"He didn't? asked Orly.

"Apparently not. Jack Grimstead was here this morning with his lawyer, that dreadful Julius Ahoel, and they were armed with a court order to examine the contents of Homer's safety deposit box. It did contain his will, which Aldwin had signed as a witness, but it was dated nine years ago. That was the only indication of the intent of the deceased. The rest of the contents of the box were the usual things—deeds, insurance policies, a beautiful silver dollar from 1922, and other keepsakes."

Palmer cleared his throat and said, "Just now, when you mentioned Jack Grimstead, you seemed to be rather, well, I mean, the tone in your voice indicated that you did not care for the man. Have you had any other relationship with him?"

Alice Monson's face began to cloud. "Yes, you might say that. He worked for us for a while, until Aldwin caught him red handed with his hand in the till –literally, he was caught with his hand in the till, trying to swipe a hundred dollar bill! As if we wouldn't notice! I wanted to prosecute, but Aldwin simply dismissed him because he liked the creep's uncle. Well, I didn't see him again until that day of the ethanol dog-and-pony show. I didn't think anything of it until Aldwin went over to make a final offer to Nora, of Nora's Knitting Nook, for her property. 'Too late,' she said. She had already sold it to 'that nice young man,' Jack Grimstead, who was going to continue the business. Well, you can imagine how I felt about that. I asked Aldwin how Jack Grimstead had got hold of the information that we were buying property for the expansion of the bank, and he admitted that he had told Homer Grimstead about it. 'I mean, Homer's been my friend for years, and I was just so danged'—yes, Aldwin actually used the word 'danged'—'proud of it that I had to tell him.' When I asked him if Jack Grimstead was listening then, he acknowledged that he probably was. Needless to say, I was not happy.

"In any event, Aldwin went over to talk to Jack Grimstead and finally made a deal with that weasel. You know, we ended up paying a lot more to him than we would have to Nora, but when it came down to it, we would have gone a lot higher. That was the last property on the block. Jack Grimstead was supposed to be a real estate man, but I don't think he quite realized the extent to which he had us over a barrel. Or not, I don't know. He did say that he could have asked for much more but that he didn't want to be greedy, etc. etc. So we paid up and Jack was on the way to a fortune."

The sheriff was puzzled. "What do you mean, 'on the way to a fortune.'

"Well, you see, that's why today was so important. Jack Grimstead bought the Knitting Nook before his uncle died. It was a big deal for him at the time. But after today, he will be a lot richer. Our studies have revealed that the ideal location for the ethanol plant would be those eighty acres that were the subject to the dispute between the hunters and the bird watchers and who knows who else. Homer and everybody else thought the land was next to worthless. But in fact, it's located in a place with virtually unlimited water supply, and a place where waste water and bi-products can be contained. It's an ideal location in terms of transportation, since it is near an entrance to the interstate, which is vital not only for the delivery of corn and whatever other organic material we'll utilize but is also necessary for the shipping of the final product. It'll meet all the environmental protection regulations. In short, we are prepared to offer that slimeball Jack Grimstead a lot of money for his property, after which we'll probably let the hunters and the bird watchers enjoy the majority of the property in perpetuity."

"Ah, well, that certainly clears things up, and to the benefit of almost everybody," said the sheriff as he prepared to stand. Orly, who like Thurber got nervous in banks, was already zipping up his jacket. It had been an enlightening conversation, but Palmer couldn't help thinking, "No wonder this bank is making so much money. It can't afford to offer a guy a cup of coffee."

As Alice Monson also stood, she said, "Benefit everybody, maybe, but especially Jack Grimstead."

LATER IN THE AFTERNOON, when the sheriff got back to his office, he noticed a young woman and a boy sitting on the couch in the reception area just outside his office. Just as he was taking off his jacket, the deputy on duty at the front desk called him and asked if he had time to see a Mrs. Lola Mattson and her son. Feeling as though he had at least cleared up the Grimstead business, Palmer thought a nice domestic problem might be refreshing. "Yah, send 'em in," he said.

The door opened cautiously and a woman with mousy-brown short hair peeked through. Over her shoulder she said, "Now you just wait right there until I come and get you, you hear me?" She stepped into the sheriff's office and closed the door. "My name is Lola Mattson, and I want you to have a word with my son."

Palmer, who had risen when she entered, indicated a chair and said, "All right, I'll see what I can do. Please sit down and tell me about it."

The woman did as she was told, and then took a deep breath. "I would like for you to pretend to arrest my son for the underage smoking of cigarettes."

Knutson hid a smile. In the midst of the most difficult case of his career, this promised to be an uncomplicated diversion. "Well, you know, technically, there's no law against underage smoking. There is certainly a law against *selling* tobacco products to minors, but, as far as I know, there is no law in any state making it illegal for a kid to smoke. What's his name, and how old is he?"

"His name's Kyle, and he's eleven years old."

"The sheriff smiled and said, "I think that's how old I was when my pals and I had our first smoke. I don't think any of us turned out too bad."

"Yes, I know what you mean, although," she smirked, "I was at least in high school. The thing is, I just want him to be aware of the dangers involved and I don't want him to think it's cool. He hangs around with two other kids in the neighborhood, and they're all involved. I've talked to the mothers of the other boys, and they just sort of laughed it off and said they'd have a little talk with their boys. I don't think poisoning children is funny," she added, primly.

Knutson realized he was in no position to claim that humor was inherent in underage smoking. "No, no, of course not. How did you find out about this, and do you know where they got the cigarettes? "

"My son Kyle came home from being with Johnny MacLarnan and Aaron Smemo. I didn't think he looked too good. I went up and gave him a hug. And I smelt it! I've got a good nose, and I smelt it. It didn't take me long to get the whole story. He said they have a little club house—he wouldn't tell me where—and that they got together and smoked. He said that Aaron Smemo had found them on the sidewalk while he was picking up his papers for delivery, and brought them back to share with his friends. Hummph. Some friend."

"Now, now, Mrs. Mattson. Don't be so hard on the kid. Your son seems like a good kid, and I think I know at least one of those kid's dads. I think they come from good homes. I'll tell you what I'll do. You send him in here, and I'll have a little talk with him about smoking. But I won't threaten him with arrest. How does that sound?"

"Hmmmm, I suppose you might know best. All right." With this Mrs. Mattson rose and called her son into the office.

Palmer put on his most stern expression, the kind he had used with his own children when the situation called for it. "So, are you Kyle Mattson?"

The poor kid shrank down into his jacket and mumbled a barely audible, "Yes, sir."

"I understand you've been smoking."

"Yes, sir."

"Do you know what might happen to you if you continue to smoke cigarettes?"

Little Kyle, looking scared, said, "No, sir."

"You won't grow strong and healthy. You'll never play for the Twins or the Vikings, and you'll probably not even grow up to be a sheriff. Do I make myself clear?"

"Yes, sir."

"Now, that's the only warning I'm going to give you. For now! And I want you to tell your friends about what I've said, and that if any of you find another pack of cigarettes, you will put them straight into the garbage can where they belong. Can you promise me that?"

"Oh, yes, sir," said Kyle, realizing at last that he was not facing major jail time.

"All right then," said the sheriff, smiling. I'm sure you have homework to do, and maybe you can even clean up your room and help your mother with supper."

"Yes, sir, I will."

The sheriff raised himself up to his highest stature and said, "Mrs. Mattson, I think we are done here. I trust we won't meet again under these circumstances."

"I'm sure we won't sheriff, will we Kyle?"

"Oh no, I promise."

As they left the room, Lola Mattson turned and looked over her shoulder, grinned, and mouthed a "Thank you, thank you," before she went out the door.

"Another case closed," thought Palmer, who decided that he had done enough for the day.

Chapter Eighteen

PALMER HAD BEEN LOOKING FORWARD to this night. The Twins were on TV. It was only two weeks into the season, and already they were two games below five hundred, but the Twins had a good young staff with good arms, and they were sure to turn things around. Ellie, a good fan in her own right, had watched the first four innings, but had then gone upstairs to watch *Grey's Anatomy*. It seemed a little cold in the house, so Palmer had put on his favorite thick terry cloth robe.

He was just sitting there, minding his own business and occasionally disagreeing with the umpire when he heard a loud thump on his front door. "Bald headed Moses!" he muttered, "What in the world was that?" He waited for a few seconds, and hearing nothing more, he tried to ignore it. But his curiosity got the better of him, and as the inning was over, he got up to check it out. He opened the door and noticed a flier from the local pizza purveyor sticking in the storm door. As he reached to take it out, it fluttered onto the steps. He groaned, stepped all the way out, and bent down to pick it up.

In this position, with his posterior elevated to the sky, his eye caught sight of a flash of flame and at the same instant a tremendous noise rang out. He toppled headfirst onto the lawn and looked back to see that a huge hole had been blasted into his front door. His second of confusion was replaced by terror and panic. "My God, someone's shooting at me!" He heard, rather than saw, a car speed away.

His heart was pounding such as it had never done before. He had never been shot at in his life, and, in fact, could not ever remember a gun other than a water pistol ever being pointed at him. He was aware of screaming, and once he determined that it wasn't him, he heard Ellie pounding down the steps. She saw him spread out on the lawn and ran to him.

"Palmer, Palmer, Palmer. Oh, Palmer. Are you alive?"

In the days to come, at a calmer moment, he realized that this was a question he had never been asked, and rather hoped to avoid in the future. Now he slowly turned and said, "Yes, I think so. In fact, I don't think I'm hurt at all. But, my God, look what they did to our door!"

"The door! Is that all you can think about? Somebody just tried to kill you." Ellie was shaking and sobbing and then giggled "I can get a new door. Getting a new husband would be the hard part!" They held each other tightly, as Ellie continued sobbing and Palmer was overcome with violent shaking. After a few minutes, during which people began to look out of doors all along the street and began to cautiously make their way over to the Knutson residence, Palmer stood up to take stock and to restore order. "Folks." he announced in a shaky voice, "we've just had a shooting incident. It's all over now. I'm okay. Just go back to your houses. Whoever did this is gone now. We might have to check in with each of you to see if you noticed anything, but everything is okay. It's okay. You're all safe. I have to go in and call for assistance."

He bravely strode back into the house, noting the extent of the damage to the door that had just been put in a year ago. Curiously, the thought crossed his mind, *I wonder if insurance would cover that? It should.*

As he hit speed dial to Orly's apartment, he marveled as to how calm he seemed to be. Orly answered with a rather bored, "Yeah, Orly Peterson here. Who's this?"

"Orly, this is Palmer. I've just been shot at."

"Shot at!" Orly choked. "Where? When? Are you all right? Who did it?"

"Well, that's for us to find out. I just stepped outside of the house for a second and someone took a shot at me with a shotgun. Blew away most of my door! I had just bent down to pick up one of those hateful fliers that that pizza joint is always passing around and Woomph!—it just missed me. But I have no idea who— all I heard was the blast and a car drive away. I guess I really didn't have the presence of mind to chase after him and get a license number or anything. So listen, get a few deputies and check with the Fergus Falls police department and . . ."

At this moment, Ellie screamed again. "Palmer! You've been hit! You're bleeding!"

The sheriff looked at her as though she had lost all of her senses until she said, "Look!"

Palmer looked in the direction of her point to see that the back of his robe was stained with blood. He took off the robe and noticed a circular blood stain in the seat of his pants. He calmly added to Orly, "It looks like you'll have to take over when you get here. The door, such as it is, will not be locked. Now, if you would excuse me, I'm on my way to the emergency ward. Apparently I have been shot."

As he looked for the keys for the Acura, Ellie said, "What do you think you're doing? You can't drive yourself to the hospital. You're bleeding and you may be in shock. Give me those keys."

As they passed through the garage, Palmer grabbed a couple of car washing rags to place on the seat. He didn't want to stain his prized car. It was only when he sat down that he became aware that he was indeed in pain. Ignoring the fact that she was in the company of an officer of the law, Ellie exceeded the speed limit.

At the emergency room, the nurse on duty immediately contacted the doctor and led Palmer to an examining room. The doctor was there in seconds, and asked him to remove his trousers. He gently swabbed the wounded area and asked Palmer to lie down on the examining table. He asked calmly, "How did this happen?"

"How did it happen?" Palmer exploded. "Someone shot me!"

"All right, calm down. That was not a dumb question. Do you know what penetrated your body? Was it a bullet? Could it have been a shard of something else? Do you know what kind of gun was used?"

"How should I know what kind of gun it was? I hardly had an opportunity to see if it were a Browning or a Winchester, for Pete's sake!"

"I mean, was it an air rifle, a shotgun, or some other kind of weapon. Whatever hit you is still in there."

"Well, get it out!"

"I intend to, I'd just like to know what I'm looking for so I don't dig around in there anymore than I have to. I'd guess that's something that you can appreciate."

"Oh, yeah, sorry. It was a shotgun—most of it hit the door."

"All right, then. If we're lucky, it'll just be a shotgun pellet. If we're not lucky, it could be a piece of wood from the door—that could be nastier. Let's just have a look-see."

Five seconds later Palmer heard a single "ping" from something dropped into a metal bowl. "That's it. I got it. You'll be fine. I should be able to cover this with a simple Band-Aid. It may be sore for a couple of days, and just to be on the safe side, I'd better give you a tetanus shot. Have you had one recently?"

Palmer, who had never cared for needles, shook his head. The doctor, appreciating that one puncture of the buttocks was enough for one day, told the sheriff to put his pants back on and roll up his sleeve. As he administered the shot, he said, "Now, want to tell me what this is all about? We have to report all gunshot wounds to the authorities, you know."

"Don't you know who I am?"

"No. Am I supposed to? I just moved to Fergus Falls two months ago."

"My name is Palmer Knutson. I'm the sheriff of Otter Tail County. The authorities."

"Oh, er, glad to meet you," the doctor said, extending his hand. "I'm Doug Sand, the, uh, new doctor here."

"Glad to meet you, too," said Palmer, "although one might have wished for more favorable circumstances."

"Indeed. I'm still going to have to file a report, although, all things considered, it can probably wait. The nurse at the front desk will still need your insurance card and . . ."

At that moment, a shout came from the entrance. "Where is he? Where's the sheriff? Where have you taken him?"

Knutson said, dryly, "That would be my deputy."

Orly burst in and asked, "Sheriff! Sheriff, are you all right?"

"Yah, yah, I'll be fine. The doc just took one pellet out of my butt. I don't know how that happened, really, but I suppose one of the pellets could have ricocheted off the metal door numbers. He just put a band aid on it. Care to kiss it and make it well?"

Orly smirked. "Why not? I do it every other day. Seriously, did you see anything? Who would want to shoot you?"

"I don't know, other than some of my political opponents. I can't remember anything I've done or said to anyone lately, so I . . . uh oh."

"What?"

"Do you remember how I was quoted in the paper this morning? I implied that I knew who had killed Stover Stordahl, but that I was keeping the information to myself for the time being. Do you suppose whoever killed Stordahl just tried to shut me up permanently?"

"Of course. That's it. But that means you're still in danger."

"Oh, I doubt it. In the first place, for all the killer knows he succeeded when he took that shot at me. On the other hand, when he finds out he didn't, he should have sense enough to know that I'd tell all I know to whoever would listen."

Orly was still doubtful. "That's sounds a little like whistling in a graveyard to me. You still gotta be careful."

"Don't worry, there's nothing like escaping death through the forces of a pizza advertisement to put one on his guard. In fact, I wonder if I'll ever feel safe again. We're clearly dealing with a dangerous, desperate individual here. Did you find anything at the scene—at the scene, my house, for God's sake—that you could use?

"No. We talked to everybody all along the block, on both sides of the street. Nobody noticed a car outside or anything. I mean, why would they? It was dark, and everybody was probably watching television. A neighborhood watch is a good thing, but that hardly means that they, you know, watch. There appeared to be one area on the pavement that had been slightly discolored as if by a rapidly spinning tire, but that would do us no good. I mean, ordinary rubber on asphalt is not going to tell us anything. We did find half a brick by your front door, if that means anything."

"Ah, that was probably what he used to get me out of the house. He must have thrown the brick, got back in the car and waited for me to come out, then blasted away. That means, at the very least, that he knew who I was. Anything distinctive about the brick?"

"A brick is a brick. We'll take it in and have it analyzed, of course, just in case he drooled on it or scraped his hand while throwing it, but I'm pretty sure we can rule out getting any evidence from that."

Knutson smiled, "All right, Orly, this is what I want you to do. Examine every structure and dump in town to find out if there is a brick missing, and then locate every shotgun in Otter Tail County and test if it's been fired in the past few hours."

For one second, Orly thought Knutson was serious. Then he said, "Right, Sheriff. I'll get right on it. You do know, however, that this is going to make news."

"Yah, but it doesn't have to make the news *tonight*. I just want to go home and go to bed. I think I'll sleep on my stomach tonight. By the way, you didn't hear how the game turned out did you?"

"Somehow, that didn't seem to be a priority."

Ellie said, "They won, three to one."

Knutson, somehow affronted, said, "How do you know that?"

"Well, when the doctor was giving you that shot, I assumed that you were all right, and I noticed that I had gotten some blood on my hands and so I went out and washed it off. As I was passing through the waiting room, the television was on, and I just paused and then they gave the score. I thought you would want to know. Palmer, can we go home now?"

As they got into the car, Palmer inspected the seats of the beloved Acura for blood. After driving in silence for a while, Ellie said, "So what are you going to do tomorrow? I don't think you should go in. There'll be reporters hanging around all day, and, I mean, if there ever was an excuse for taking the day off, you've found it."

"Maybe you're right, Ellie. I can see the headlines now. 'SHERIFF SHOT IN ASS.'"

Chapter Nineteen

I N RETROSPECT, IT PROBABLY WENT AS WELL as could be expected. Knutson had called a news conference for nine o'clock the morning after the shooting. Reporters from the twin cities and from Fargo-Moorhead were all there, as well as Tracie Ryan from the *Fergus Falls Daily Journal*. He assured them all that he had sustained only a mild wound in "the lower back" and that it was really no more than a scratch. He felt that he needed to play down the incident not only because of the sensitive nature of the wound's location, but also because the city had just experienced a murder and an attack on their sheriff. He didn't want to create any more tension in the community. He also assured them that he was eager to continue the investigation.

This last statement was not, perhaps, technically true. He had laid awake for hours, not so much because of the pain in his hinder, as he delicately referred to it when his children had called, but because he was getting nowhere in the investigation. The attack was most assuredly connected to the murder investigation, and it meant that whoever shot at him was getting nervous.

Nervous people were dangerous. No one had ever imagined that Knutson was a coward, but as he lay in bed, he began to realize that he was truly afraid. In spite of his assurances to his deputy, he realized that he could be attacked again. This led him to contemplate once again just how much longer he really wanted to be sheriff. Sleep, when it did come, was fitful and unsatisfying, filled with dreams of smoking children with shotguns.

Alone in his office after the press conference, he stared at the the map of Norway hanging on the wall. As he was concentrating on what to do next, Orly walked by the door and sang, "I shot the sheriff, but I did not shoot the deputy." This was all he sang, for, if truth be told, he did not know any more of the words. Palmer felt annoyed, but reflecting on the obvious concern that Orly had shown for him last night, was in a forgiving mood and decided to ignore it.

Ten minutes later, Orly again strolled by and again intuned, "I shot the sheriff, but I did not shoot the deputy." This time, Palmer could not let it pass and shouted, "Eric Clapton was never any good after he left Cream."

Orly stopped to ask, "What does cream have to do with anything? Did Eric Clapton eat a lot of cream?"

Palmer shook his head in disgust.

After trying to remember all the songs from his old Cream album, and thinking that he himself would have to "shoot the deputy," Palmer abruptly reached for the telephone and called Ellie. She answered and he said, "It's me."

"Oh, Palmer, I'm so glad. The phone's been ringing ever since you left. I've had reporters requesting information and even interviews. One of the papers wants to do a feature on me, 'the wife of the sheriff, who waits in terror as her husband fights evil' kind of thing. I told them to call back tomorrow. And all the relatives and friends and neighbors are caught up in the excitement of the whole thing—you wouldn't believe it!"

"Well, I probably would," admitted Palmer. "I'm getting the same thing here. I decided that I just want to take off a few hours and go home, so I won't be home for some time."

That statement would not have made sense to anyone but Palmer and Ellie. For Palmer Knutson, "home" meant the family farmstead near Underwood, Minnesota, about a dozen miles east of Fergus Falls. Palmer's grandfather had built the house and began farming shortly after he had emigrated from Norway in 1893. Now the farmstead had all but disappeared, the only evidence that this had once been a family home was a thinning line of box elders and a windmill, still standing guard over dreams and memories.

Palmer eased his way into his Acura and headed out of town. He put a CD of Saint Saens music into the dashboard player. Somehow, someway, he couldn't even remember now, he had been introduced to French Impressionist music. He would listen to *la Mer*, by Debussy, and imagine himself on a small boat in the Mediterranean sun. Today, for reasons he could not explain, *Carnival of the Animals* seemed the perfect choice.

It was almost noon when he parked the car at the end of the driveway. Perhaps he could have driven farther, but the last thing he wanted to do was to get mired in the deep ruts and plead for a neighboring farmer to use a tractor to pull him out. Besides, the road had seen wagon wheels and truck tires. He wasn't sure if there was even clearance for an automobile. He walked the hundred yards to where the lawn once started. It had been his job to mow it after his brother had left for college. It seemed so big, then, but now he realized that it was probably not much larger than many residential lots in the city. As he approached, the wind turned the windmill blades, and a mournful shriek shattered the absolute quiet. He walked to the place where the house once stood. Now there was nothing but a concrete lined basement, used by the current owner of the property as a place to dump field stones. The sun was warm. Palmer unzipped his jacket and found a rock on which to sit. He lowered himself gingerly and gazed at an exposed section of the concrete floor where he used to play with his wind up toy bulldozer and trucks. Hidden in perpetual shadow, there was still a trace of snow between the rocks. He began a silent conversation with himself.

"I love this place, I really do. I wonder how it looked when my Grandpa, Erik Gustav Knutson, first saw it? Was it the culmination of his dreams or was it a place 'good enough to start out with until I can find something better?'"

Palmer was the youngest son of a youngest son, so he didn't know his grandfather very well. He remembered him as a stooped, gray-haired man of whom he was just a little afraid. He did not seem to have much affection for younger children, and Palmer's parents seemed to go out of their way to assure that Grandpa was not bothered. Still, in fifth grade, Palmer's teacher had required her students to write a report on where their ancestors had come from. In Palmer's class of seventeen, there were two Swedes, one German, and fourteen Norwegians. The teacher told them that just to say they came from Norway was not enough. So Palmer had talked to Grandpa, and for the first time he showed a tender side as he told Palmer of his childhood. He died shortly afterwards.

Palmer remembered that conversation now, as he tried to imagine his grandfather as a young man. He had grown up south of Tynset, on the banks of the Gloma River and in the shadow of Tron, the highest mountain in Norway. Palmer had always wanted to go there, and, revisiting last night's sleeplessness, he contemplated retiring and doing just that. But if he went back, he would fly from Minneapolis to Oslo. Palmer reflected that he really didn't understand all that his grandfather had told him at the time, but in the years since he had learned to a greater extent what he had experienced. When he started college, and began to study history, he would often come home to talk to his father about those things that Erik Gustav had experienced.

"Think of the courage," Palmer said aloud to the old farm. "He was seventeen years old. He was practically penniless—I wonder if they ever used the term ore-less—the oldest brother got the farm. He was religiously oppressed. The local *preste* ran that community like a medieval fiefdom. No future, just guts. He got on a boat, crossed the North Sea to Hull, took a train to Liverpool, and then it was a trip across an ocean which he had never seen before. And when he came to New York, he probably saw the brand new Statue of Liberty lifting her lamp before the golden door and then went through Castle Garden processing. Then on the train across half a continent until he got to Decorah, Iowa, the distribution point for Norwegian immigration. He remembered the old joke of the Norwegian who went to New York and said, 'If this is New York, wow! I wonder what Decorah must be!' I suppose the Norwegians thought that joke was funnier than a rubber crutch! I suppose I can say that here, especially since I'm not really speaking out loud.

"Then he came up here, to what they used to call the Park Region. And built this farm. And he never went anywhere else. As far as I know, he never saw another mountain and never saw the ocean again. But he did see the ocean once, all I've seen of the the ocean was from several thousand feet in the air when they sent me to Germany when I was in the army. I wish I'd gone to college before I was in the army. I suppose I appreciated Germany about as much as any other nineteen-year-old kid who just hangs around with his buddies and drinks German beer. And Grandpa even got to see England, which is something I still haven't done. Here I am, in the middle of the continent, getting old and getting shot.

"And what for? When I started being sheriff, we'd investigate cottage break-ins, the odd shoplifting, a few domestic cases, some public drunkenness, and deliver warrants. Now what do I do? I have a whole unit that does little more than deliver warrants and judgments, and even then they have to be armed to the teeth just in case someone disagrees with them. I've got another task force that does nothing but chase down drug trafficking. Sixty percent of the inmates of my jail are methamphetamine users, and now we have to police cold remedies so they don't end up in somebody's meth lab. Somebody violently takes the life of an innocent lamb like Stover Stordahl! What's with that? Maybe it really is time to retire. Time for Matt Dillon to hang up his spurs. Did he wear spurs? Well, his hat anyway. I'd love to hear the roar of the waves on the ocean. I want to go to London and Bath and Edinburgh and York."

As Palmer thought of the sea and of England, he thought of a poem he'd memorized while in college. He did like the poem, but in those pre-Ellie days, he was drawn to a certain coed who seemed to love to talk about Matthew Arnold. He thought a good tactic to further their relationship would be to memorize *Dover Beach*. As a tactic, it was successful as far as it went, which turned out to be not very far when Palmer discovered that he understood poetry while the dizzy red head from Alexandria merely thought talking about poetry was cool.

> "The sea is calm tonight.
> The tide is full, the moon lies fair
> Upon the straits; on the French coast the light
> Gleams and is gone; the cliffs of England stand
> Glimmering and vast, out in the tranquil bay.
> Come to the window, sweet is the night air!
> Only, from the long line of spray
> Where the sea meets the moon-blanch'd land,
> Listen! you hear the grating roar
> Of Pebbles which the waves draw back, and fling
> At their return, up the high strand,
> Began, and cease, and then again began,
> With tremulous cadence slow, and bring
> Their eternal note of sadness in."

"'Eternal note of sadness.' That about says it all. Meth addicts, domestic violence, and a murder that the sheriff of Otter Tail County is supposed to solve. A sheriff who probably should just quit since he has no idea what to do next. Maybe I should just chuck the whole thing and go to see the white cliffs of Dover and gaze at the ocean and hear the 'grating roar.' As Palmer sank into self-pity, a symbol of Minnesota poked his head up from a small hole. It was a striped gopher. It took a few tentative steps toward the sheriff and then stood straight up to do his best Meerkat imitation while he observed his surroundings. Palmer sighed. He remembered his teenage days when he would drive around the country with his best friend, Stanley Nelson, slowly searching the ditches for just such prey. They would stop beside a gopher hole, roll down the window of Knutson's '53 Chevy Special, poke the Winchester .22 at the hole, and wait for him to come out. As he looked at the benign rodent now, Palmer couldn't imagine shooting the innocent creature. *Ah, those were the days,* he thought. *Stan! I wonder where he is now? There are no friendships you will ever have like the ones you have when you're fifteen years old.* He recalled how *Dover Beach* ended:

"Nor certitude, nor peace, nor help for pain;
And we are here as on a darkling plain
Swept with confused alarms of struggle and flight,
Where ignorant armies clash by night.

"Well, that's cheerful, isn't it. Ignorant armies! Led by me—a completely ignorant sheriff!"

Palmer stood and gazed around in a complete circle. "But at least here, right here, I was satisfied and happy. There's where the barn used to be, where I fed cows and helped with the milking; where I brought in hay; where I cleaned out a space at the end of the hay mow to nail a basket on the wall to play basketball. I loved that time. I always had the ball with ten imagined seconds to go in the final game of the Minnesota State High School Basketball tournament. I'd bounce the ball against the wall, to an imaginary teammate, who would always considerately pass it back to me to take the final shot. If I made it, we won the championship. If I didn't, well, that was because I was fouled. If I made my free-throw, we won the championship, if I didn't—Wait! A lane violation. Knutson will get another shot! He missed it again, but wait! Another lane violation! How often do you see that, folks? This shot could do it and the crowd is going wild!'

"And over there, well, that was where the granary was. I'd hang an inner tube on the wall at just the right height, and that would be home plate. I'd pace off a reasonable estimate for the distance to the pitcher's mound, go into my windup and throw strikes in the center of the inner tube. It was always the bottom of the ninth, bases loaded, and the most dangerous New York Yankee of them all, Mickey Mantle, at the plate. If, as it happened far too often, I would hit the inner tube, well, then it would be a ground ball, and I'd hustle over and pick it up and try to make a play at the plate. Why was I always so much better when I'd throw against the granary than I was when I had to do something while the coach was watching?

"And there, right between the barn and the chicken coop, was my gridiron. Oh, those wonderful Saturday afternoons, when the corn was picked and the beans were harvested and I could listen to the Golden Gophers on my little black transistor radio. They were golden, too, back then, anyway. But I always thought that the missing ingredient to a trip to the Rose Bowl was Knutson at quarterback. I'd throw the ball in a spiral high into the air and then become a glue fingered end who would make the catch for a touchdown.

"Looking back on it, I suppose some people would find that pathetic. A lonely farm boy playing catch with himself. I probably knew deep down that I'd never make the major leagues or play for the Gophers, but for a few hours I did. And that made all the difference. And what do kids do now? They waste their time and rot their minds with video games. I think I'd take my imagination over somebody else's imaginary video adventures every time. For one thing, I always won.

"I suppose it was lonely, at times, and I would have liked to have been able to get together with a couple of other guys after school like Kyle Mattson." Palmer smiled as he recalled his conversation with the boy and his mother. Kids trying out their first cigarette! It was a shame, of course, and the American tobacco companies had a lot to answer for, but as long as there were mothers like Mrs. Mattson, well, Kyle should be all right. He remembered the first time he had tried a cigarette. It was at the church midsummer picnic. Some guy had dropped a Winston in the grass and an older kid found it. He found matches in the glove compartment of his father's car and four boys sneaked into the woods behind the church and lit up. As Palmer remembered it, nobody really liked it, but all agreed it was a fine thing to do. What was his name again? Myron, that was it, Myron Johnson. I suppose it was like that when that friend of Kyle Mattson's found that pack of cigarettes and—"

And suddenly Palmer thought of what he had been thinking from the moment when Stover Stordahl's body was discovered. Could it be? Could he really get lucky in this investigation at last? The sheriff stood and purposefully strode back to his car.

As the sheriff made his way back to Fergus Falls, other minds in the community were wrestling with their own thoughts.

"It wasn't my fault. He was asking for it. How was I to know about that whole Tourette's Syndrom thing. I mean, it was hardly my fault."

"We gotta have that land. I pretty much went out on a limb there. No sappy bird watching wimps got a right to it. Old Homer meant for us to have it."

" I should never have taken the shot at the sheriff. I mean, the first thing was sort of an accident. Man-slaughter, really. But this was premeditated attempted murder. There really is no way out. Maybe I should just hop in the car and go to Canada. I could just go out I-94, go to Fargo, get on I-29, and in three hours I could be over the border. Winnepeg is a nice town."

"When it comes right down to it, I guess I really don't care whether they shoot the prairie chickens or not. But it's the principle of the thing. If there's one thing I do, it's lead. I must be out in front on this."

"I wonder how much that weasel is going to demand for that land? If he thinks I'll be as much of a softie as Aldwin was, he's got another think coming."

"So, everything is all set, and the Congressman is proud of me. Problem solved. Moreover, I rather think that this puts me in his debt. He won't be able to get rid of me, and I can ride him all the way into the big leagues of Washington."

"I'm never, never, never gonna smoke another cigarette."

Chapter Twenty

DEPUTY ORLY PETERSON KNOCKED on the sheriff's door and entered at the same time, a practice that had annoyed Knutson for ages, but one which he had always accepted with forebearance. "Did you bring him in?"

Knutson sat before a mound of administrative paperwork, but was studiously avoiding it while he planned ahead for the interview. "Yah, I took Chuck Schultz along with me. I didn't think there would be any trouble, and there wasn't, but one can't be too sure in a case like this. He seemed a little nervous, but he tried to act as though he had nothing to be nervous about. I put him in the interview room about forty minutes ago. I figure it doesn't hurt to let him stew a bit."

"Have you arrested him?"

"Arrested? Ha! I haven't a scrap of evidence. Unless he gives us something, we can't even hold him overnight."

Orly asked, "So, how do you want to play it?"

"Good cop—bad cop, you mean? Well, I had talked to him earlier in the week, and we actually got along pretty well. I suppose you can be the bad cop, as usual."

"What do you mean, 'as usual?'"

"I just think with all your spit and polish and uniformed efficiency you can do a better job of threatening them with the law. I meant it as a compliment."

"Oh, well, all right then. I'll let you start and when the time seems right, I'll go for the jugular, 'as usual.'"

⁕ ⁕

THEY ENTERED THE INTERVIEW ROOM to see a very distraught Jack Grimstead leaning over the table with his head in his hands. He looked up anxiously.

"All right, Jack, since this is a formal interview, we will be recording it. Do you wish to have a lawyer present?"

"Why would I need a lawyer? Grimstead sputtered.

Peterson glared at him and said: "Yes, well, it may be that you will need a lawyer very soon." He prepared the recorder with a fresh tape, noted the time and date, and said: "This recording is being made in the interview room of the Otter Tail County Law Enforcement Center. Present are Sheriff Palmer Knutson, Jack Grimstead, and myself, Chief Deputy Orly Petertson. Mr. Grimstead has been advised of his right to have an attorney present. He has declined."

With the tape rolling, Knutson waited a few moments and then said, "Now, Mr. Grimstead, I wish to discuss with you the matter of certain real estate dealings that you have had over the past month."

A look of fear mixed with a slight tinge of relief spread across Grimstead's face. "Well, all right," he said, "what do you want to know?"

Palmer smiled and said, "It seems that you were able to acquire property on the downtown block dominated by Fergus Falls First Federal, to wit, the business establishment called 'Nora's Knitting Nook.' Is that right?"

"Yes, that's correct."

"When we discussed this at an earlier date, you told me that you had simply heard a rumor as to the bank's expansion, and proceeded to make what you considered to be a wise and timely investment."

"Er, yes, that's how it happened."

"We have come into information that this may not have been true. Would you like to amend you statement?"

Grimstead eyed the sheriff suspicially for a while, before finally throwing up his hands and saying, "All right, it wasn't quite like that. I had gone into the bank with my uncle Homer. We met with Aldwin Monson about my uncle's somewhat vague idea about willing some land to that hunting club, whatever they call it, the one that's led by Chief Foss. Well, they talk it over for a while—I'm not sure just why my uncle decided to drag me along in any event. It wasn't any business of mine. So, anyway, old Monson starts bragging about how he has been doing so well lately, getting the financing for that ethanol plant and everything, and then he starts telling my uncle about his big plans. He shows us his plans to acquire the whole block and to double the size of the bank. I could see right away that he would need to acquire Nora's Knitting Nook—it's right in the middle of the block. I mean, I'm in the real estate business, and even if I wasn't, well, it wouldn't take a rocket scientist to see that he needed to get that property and would have to pay whatever he needed to in order to get it. Inside information? Sure. But there's nothing illegal about it. Besides, I used to work in that bank and I didn't particularly care for old man Monson. I gotta admit that I enjoyed getting a little of my own back at him."

"So you went to Nora and . . ."

"I talked to her real nice, kind of laid on the charm, and I found out what Monson was offering her for her building. I offered her two thousand more, and I told her I'd give her an extra thousand for her inventory. She assumed, although I never did promise, that I'd be taking over the business and all of her loyal customers could still get their yarn and whatever else they needed from me. We got on like a house afire after that, and I got my lawyer and my financing in order and bought it the next day. Just like that. Nothing illegal about that."

"Maybe not, but you did turn around and sell it for a good profit?"

"Of course, I had Monson over a barrel. So what? There's no crime in making a profit."

"Of course not," Knutson agreed, "sounds like a shrewd, if somewhat underhanded business deal. But, of course, that isn't what really concerns us."

"Er . . . no? Then what's the problem?"

Orly leaned forward with his face only inches from Grimstead's. It was time for the "bad cop" to go into his act. Summoning up what he considered to be his steely expression, he said in a menacing voice, "It's what you did after you took possession. How in the world did you think you could get by with that? You had to know that the truth would come out! We have plenty of evidence of what you did. You're really not a very accomplished criminal are you! It's almost insulting to think that you could fool anybody. I'll tell you this, however. If you confess and tell us all about it, well, maybe some sort of deal with the prosecutor can be made. We can't promise anything, we just enforce the law, we don't decide sentences. But in most cases, a guilty plea results in a somewhat reduced sentence. Sure, we can sit here and play cat and mouse all night, and we will sit here as long as it takes, but the game's up, and you might as well tell us about it!"

Grimstead looked pleadingly at Knutson. The eyes seemed to say, "How can you let him talk to me this way? I thought we were friends." The sheriff studiously stared at a corner of the ceiling, then methodically clicked and unclicked a ball point pen. Finally Knutson, in a quiet, reassuring voice that seemed to imply that he was Grimstead's only friend, said "He's right, you know. We know what you've committed a crime. *You* know you committed a crime. It would just be easier for everybody if it all came out now."

Grimstead stared at his hands as though seeing them for the first time. He studied his shoes and the clock on the wall. He looked from Peterson to Knutson in turn. The only sound was the clicking of the sheriff's pen. At last he said, "I never meant to commit a crime when I bought that building. It was only later when the idea came to me. And really, it was so easy."

Knutson asked, "Are you sure you wouldn't like your lawyer present?"

Grimstead looked somewhat relieved as he leaned back and said, "No, that's all right. I'm not even sure if I could have gone through with it. It was my uncle's wish to give away that land and, whatever becomes of it, whether it's sold for the ethanol plant or whether it just stays a nature preserve, well, it's what he wanted. What the heck, I got his old Cadillac, right?"

"It's not a bad car you know," Knutson told him with a smile. "It's hardly broken in, and all you have to do is drive it for a few years and you can sell it to a collector."

"Yeah, maybe I'll do that. Anyway, here's what happened. I did go with my uncle to the bank, and I was very aware of what he wanted to do. Old Monson promised to help him with some of the paperwork, and in the meantime he'd do a little checking on his own. But my uncle wanted to make sure that his wishes were made known, so both Monson and I signed a rather crude form of a will. Had Monson not died just after my uncle, he would've told you that. So, I go with my uncle down to the basement to put the new will in his safety deposit box. We're in there all alone and he says 'I got a lucky box. The combination number is 922. I was born in 1922, so I can never forget it.' As he was stuffing the will in his box, I had a look around. I had worked there before, you know, only I was now seeing the bank in connection with a possible real estate deal. It occurred to me at the time that the property that Monson wanted to buy was just on the other side of the basement wall. I even noticed a ventilating grill in the corner and wondered if the whole building would have to be gutted and modernized for new heating and air conditioning. But then, I really didn't think of anything beyond that, I was thinking more about how I could scrape up the capital to buy Nora's Knitting Nook.

"Well, you know all about that. I bought the place and was in the process of liquidating all of the stock I had taken over from Nora. Anyway, so just last week— a week ago today, as it turns out—it was the day that Aldwin Monson died. Wow! It seems like a hundred years ago! My uncle had died the day before and I knew I'd have to sort that out. Anyway, just last week I thought I'd look in the basement of Nora's Nook to see if I could find any boxes. It turned out that there was hardly anything down there, but I was scrounging around to see if there was anything I could use. I did find a couple of cardboard boxes, however, and so I turned out the light and started back up the stairs. Just then, though, I noticed a little ray of light coming from the far corner. 'Curious', I thought, 'I wonder where that's coming from.' I investigated and found that there was a back vent that went into some kind of tunnel. I got a flashlight and shined it through the grill and discovered that there was a small tunnel that carried heating pipes. Then I remembered Monson once boring me to death when I was working in the bank, with stories about how the building used to be heated by an old fashioned steam boiler and that coal trucks used to dump coal down a shoot for the boiler every winter and the resulting steam heat was ever so much more pleasant and healthy than the forced air gas furnace that heated the place now. All right, fine, so what? But when I turned off the flashlight, I was able to determine that the light that I'd seen was coming from another vent and it dawned on me that it would have to be the vent in the safety deposit box room in the bank. At the time I just shook my head. That had to be the most stupid lack of security I had ever seen, but typical of Aldwin Monson.

"To tell you the truth, however, it did not enter my head until the next day that I could use that entry to get into the bank. I already knew the combination to the safety deposit box, of course, and I just started to amuse myself about how easy it would be to just go in and open the box and remove the will. Other than my uncle, the only one who knew of its existence was Monson, and he had just shuffled through the pearly gates, too. It was just innocent musing at the time, of course, but as Saturday wore on, I had convinced myself that I could do it. As you know, Sheriff, I took Roxanne Dahl out for supper that night. It wasn't totally unpleasant, because I could let my mind wonder to what I would do once I got rid of her. I thought I would have to act fast, before anybody else decided that the safety deposit box should be opened and what better time than a dark April Saturday night? Downtown would be deserted, and, in the event anybody saw me in Nora's Knitting Nook, well, it was my building and I had a perfect right to be there.

"So, you know the rest, I suppose. After I took Roxanne home, I went back to my place to put on my grubbiest jeans and a sweat shirt because I knew it would be filthy down there, and it was. So I went to Nora's Nook, now my Nook, I suppose, and parked right in front.

I went right down to the basement and checked out the situation. There was just enough room for me to take my flashlight, slip through the vent on my side, and make my way to the bank vent. Now, this was the tricky part. I wasn't even sure if I could push out that vent and get in. I mean, I could hardly start banging away and make it all too apparent that I had broken in. I brought along a crow bar, but instead I just cautiously pushed against the inside of the back vent and it gave way immediately. It had been nailed in place into ordinary sheetrock, and the nails stuck out an inch on the other side. Since it was a baseboard vent, all I had to do was push it out. It didn't even make a noise. Again, the size of the opening was just right. I crawled through, found my uncle's box, opened it up, took the will, which was right on the top, and locked it back up again.

"Then I looked down on the floor. One cannot climb through old tunnels on one's hands and knees and not leave a mark. And besides, I had to figure out how to get the vent grill back in place. I reasoned that I had all night, however, so I went back to Nora's little knitting store and found all the right cleaning supplies, and then I was able to solve the problem of getting the grill back in place. After I cleaned the area around the safety deposit boxes, I used a pair of pliars to bend back the nails that had held the grill in place. I looped wire through the nails, threaded each wire through the nail hole, crawled back into the tunnel, and carefully pulled the nails through. In order to keep it tight, I tied the wires together on the opposite side. I figured that when they tore up the whole thing for the bank expansion, nobody would be too interested in that, or maybe they would just shake their heads about the slipshod way they did things in the old days.

"I realize I've committed a felony for breaking and entering the bank. Again, I don't know if my conscience would have let me keep the money from the sale of that land anyway. In a way, its a relief. I've been thinking of nothing else since that night. I suppose I'll have to serve some time in jail, or maybe since it's the first offense I could get some sort of probation?"

Grimstead looked at Peterson, who grimly shook his head.

"Anyway, that's the whole story. I did steal the will, but I'm willing to testify now as to my uncle's intentions." Grimstead took a long breath and sighed in relief. He looked at the sheriff and his deputy with hope in his eyes.

Knutson did not respond. He stared at Grimstead for two minutes, then four, during which Knutson kept rythmically clicking his pen, staring at Grimstead with pitiless contempt. After five minutes, Grimstead said, "Um, . . . um, . . . I, . . . er. . . . um," and then again lapsed into silence. Five more agonizing minutes passed, during which nothing could be heard but the ominous clicking. A bead of sweat fell from the tip of Grimstead's nose. Peterson remained absolutely still. At last, Knutson thought, *It's now or never. I have not a shred of evidence, no murder weapon, no motive, and only a suspicion. Yet, I know it's true.* He quietly said: "When you came back from stealing the will, was that when you killed Stover Stordahl?"

Jack Grimstead turned white. He started to shake and did not notice the drool that had oozed from the side of his mouth. After another long silence, he breathed out a barely audible "Yes."

After another long silence, Knutson looked into Grimstead's eyes with pity and a pain that he felt in the very bowels of his being. "Tell us about that," he gently said.

"Murder was the farthest thing from my mind. I've always avoided violence. I never even played football in high school because I hated the idea that I might hurt someone even more than I hated the idea of getting hurt myself. I could never stand hunting because I didn't want to hurt animals. I joined the bird watcher's society because, well, that's just my nature. That's how I got to know Stover.

"That Saturday night, just as I was coming out of that tunnel with my tools, a flashlight, and my uncle's will in my hand, there stood Stover. I stared at him dumbly and he just smiled and said that he was taking a walk around town and had seen the light on in my new business. He just walked in—My God ! I hadn't even shut the door properly!—and he said he heard noises in the basement and decided to go down to see what I was doing. Talk about being caught with your hand in the cookie jar. I had the crow bar in my hand, and as he took an interested look around my little basement, I hit him. It wasn't anything planned. I didn't think to kill him. I just hit him out of frustration more than anything else. As you know, he wasn't a large man, and that one blow killed him. At least, I thought it did. The story in the newspaper speculated that maybe he died later. If I had thought that he was still alive, I would have taken him to the hospital. I'm sure I would have."

"It was like someone else was acting and I was watching. I calmly cleaned up the basement, packed him in a bag, and hauled him upstairs. I remember thinking how light he was. I looked out, and the street was deserted. My car—actually, I was driving my uncle's Cadillac that night since I had been out on a date—was right in front of the door. I opened the trunk, went back in and picked up Stover, and dumped him in. Certainly if anybody had been about at that time of the night, they would have seen me, but no one ever is. I decided to take him out of town and dump the body, after I made sure that I had left no traces. I drove as far as Rothsay, and thinking that was far enough, I dumped him out.

Orly quietly asked, "So there was no significance in the fact that you dumped him under the prairie chicken?"

"What do you mean?"

"He was a bird watcher. Saturday was the day of the big prairie chicken outing."

"Huh? Oh, that's right. I guess I never thought about that."

Orly asked, "What did you do with the murder weapon?"

"When I got back to town, I just walked over to the bridge and tossed it in the river. I can show you approximately where it landed."

Palmer scraped his chair back and stood. "Jack Grimstead, I arrest you for the murder of John Stordahl. You have the right to remain silent. Anything you say can and will be held against you in a court of law. You have the right to an attorney. If you cannot afford an attorney, one will be provided for you. Do you under-stand the charges?"

For the murderer, relief had replaced fear. He stood and said, "Yes, sir. My attorney is Julius Ahoel. May I call him now?"

Knutson said in an official manner, "Deputy Peterson, see that Mr. Grimstead is able to telephone his lawyer." And with that, he began to leave the room.

Before he could go far, however, the murderer, said, "Excuse me, Sheriff, I just want to, you know, er, apologize for trying to shoot you the other night. Um, nothing personal. I just assumed, from what you told the press, that you knew I'd done it, and I guess I thought it was the only way out."

Knutson felt nothing but contempt for the killer, but it occurred to him that this was an apology that he was unlikely to receive again. He actually mumbled a "That's all right," and started to open the door.

But Grimstead had one more question. "Sheriff? How did you know? I thought I had taken every precaution. What evidence did I leave behind?"

Knutson, in a manner that belied the significance of his discovery earlier that afternoon, said: " A couple of days ago I had the duty of warning a sixth-grade boy about the dangers of smoking. It seems that he and two friends had gotten together for a little smoke. They could not keep this little adventure from their parents. Apparently, one of the boys had found an almost full package of cigarettes downtown when he went to pick up the Sunday papers. I didn't see any significance in this at the time.

"But I always believed that, if I could determine where Stover Stordahl had been attacked, I'd know who killed him. But how was I to discover that? This afternoon, I was thinking about those kids and it occurred to me that few people discard an almost full pack of cigarettes. If they do, they're determined to quit and thus make a ritual of throwing them in a garbage can.

Then it hit me. Who was the most notable smoker in all of Fergus Falls? Well, in my mind, it was Stover Stordahl.

"Now, could it be that those cigarettes were Tareytons? If so, they would almost certainly be Stover's. I contacted the kid who found them, and he not only confirmed that they were indeed Tareytons, but he took me to the exact place where he had found them. They had been found directly in front of Nora's Knitting Nook. Stover cherished those Tareytons, and he would never have willingly left them in front of your store. Apparently from what you have just told us, the Tareytons fell out of the bag as you put poor Stover in the trunk."

Grimstead looked puzzled and merely said, "Oh."

THE SETTING SUN STREAMED into the office of the Otter Tail County Sheriff. Knutson gingerly sat down at his desk. His "hinder" hurt worse than ever. He called Stacie Ryan and without enthusiasm outlined what had just occurred in the interview room and told her if she had additional qustions she could ask them at tomorrow's press conference. He scanned his desk for forgotten chores and long ignored paperwork. After a long and introspecitve wheeze, he signed the papers that officially entered him into the race for re-election for sheriff. Then it was time to go home.

THE END

About the Author

Dr. Gerald Anderson is a native of Hitterdal, Minnesota and a former award winning professor of history at North Dakota State University. This is the third of his series of mystery novels featuring the fictional Palmer Knutson, sheriff of Ottertail County. He currently resides in Rochester, Minnesota. Previous titles in this series are *Death Before Dinner* (2007) and *Murder Under the Loon* (2008).